T0171693

Paradox and Rebirth

A Novel

Ron Prasad

iUniverse, Inc.
New York   Bloomington

Paradox and Rebirth
A Novel

iUniverse books may be ordered through booksellers or by contacting:

iUniverse
1663 Liberty Drive
Bloomington, IN 47403
www.iuniverse.com
1-800-Authors (1-800-288-4677)

ISBN: 978-1-4401-9127-5 (sc)
ISBN: 978-1-4401-9129-9 (dj)
ISBN: 978-1-4401-9128-2 (ebk)

Printed in the United States of America

iUniverse rev. date: 11/11/2009

For my girls, without whom I couldn't have become a man.
Cindy, Reena, and Seema Prasad.

And for those who have always walked alongside my path, who have remained human beings in the truest sense, even if it hurts sometimes. And because their brilliance is my only reason to believe there may actually be a God.
Cee-lo Green, Maynard James Keenan, Esthero, Chris Cornell, Tupac Shakur, Stevie Wonder, Stephen King, Bob Marley, Peter Gabriel, Everlast, and Dante Alighieri.

Part I

A Dream of Paradox

Prologue

Sitting with her arms crossed atop the windowsill, she peered into the streets below; a half-worn red crayon clutched firmly in her left hand. Perhaps some inspiration was being sought in the scene outside. The artwork was concealed on the blank page beneath her crossed elbows for the right moment to expose itself, waiting for the insight to come to her. The lines of the sketch would eventually materialize in her head and speak through her hand, becoming a coherent image little by little. Of course, the artwork itself had always existed on that particular piece of paper, waiting for a precise moment to show itself, and only she had the power to release it.

Art was like that—as most artists, writers, and musicians already knew. All of the experiences in one's entire lifetime, a generation, and beyond even that—perhaps since the beginning of time—would combine together to create a completely new blueprint for thought. These ideas and experiences caused the universe to come to a screeching halt the moment the pen made first contact with a sheet of paper, and new life was born. Its lifespan was unknown. Some pieces lasted centuries, and some a mere few seconds. Despite this, the chance must still be taken. If you were lucky enough, a finished work of art would sit in front of you after many hours, or days, or years of work—fathered by knowledge and experience, and mothered by thought, creativity, and action. She didn't know it yet because she was young, but she'd figure it out someday. She was a smart girl.

Their time together was always short, and in fact, she was unaware of his existence at all. He didn't know her name, how old she might be, or even who her mother was. You see, that was his problem; he didn't

3

know much of anything at that point. He was determined to learn if there was any hope in that. Although he knew nothing *of* her, Cirrus Jacobs knew exactly *who* she was.

The open window blew a soft gust of wind above her head and sent a few strands waving in his direction. Although they seemed to be calling, Cirrus could only enjoy those precious moments they shared together in silence and without movement. It was only when he attempted to make contact, that the connection itself was severed. When he was in *that* place, the synaptic currents that ran between the cells of his brain burned hotter and faster than anything imaginable.

Some kind of awakening had begun to spread throughout his mind like a virus, and as a result, Cirrus Jacobs's life was lived in paradox. Like liquid magma that churned and boiled violently within the earth's center, as did spirituality within the sentient being.

He had found the landscape in which this sanctuary resided, and he had dubbed it *Paradoxum.* He had read that word once in a poem that he could not recall. Latin for *paradox.* When Cirrus Jacobs came upon his place of peace for the very first time, that word had resonated within his every cell. And he knew immediately he was home.

It was a place where existence had no physical sense, where time remained unmeasured. Paradoxum lived within the deepest recesses of the mind, where one went to hope. To travel there was effortless. It was the place you went to dream, to desire, to process logic, and to reason. It was a matter of closing the eyes and allowing for the natural drift. This mystic place could be encountered during deep sleep when rapid eye movement occurred, or in moments when emotion reigned supreme over intellect. It was the place two people visited together when they were locked in each other's embrace. A place that became visible at moments when intense heat was generated between two bodies that breathed in complete unison, becoming one.

The truth was, Cirrus Jacobs was quite an ordinary man. Actually, less than ordinary, and life had become less than satisfactory in the confines of his everyday life. He didn't know how close to insanity he may have been, because sometimes he could feel his grip slipping. Nevertheless, he'd chosen not to stay any longer. His place was not in what most so ignorantly referred to as *the real world*; it was in Paradoxum, and he'd chosen to pursue his path toward residing there permanently. Paradoxum was where his meaning could be found, and the movement proved crucial.

A battle had been waged inside his mind and it encapsulated his soul … if there was such a thing. Countless soldiers stood fearless on opposing sides, and he, with one foot on either side of the scale, was centered in balance. Only two words could describe these separate crusaders: *light* and *darkness*.

It was the most classic of all philosophical conflicts, and he was torn in two between them. Each side would need to fight increasingly stronger and faster than their rivals. It was ultimately his decision which would prevail, because it was his reason and logic that was to be their reward. Cirrus himself would struggle to balance equilibrium because his lack of resistance would surely shroud him with darkness.

To reach the enlightenment of light, one had to struggle. To embrace the blackness, one only had to let go.

This was not merely Cirrus Jacobs's battle; it occurred in every human being at some time or another and it was imperative to be able to identify it. He had opened his eyes and witnessed their combat in the physical world. Their struggle was ubiquitously evident. Wherever there was a spectrum of light trying to illuminate an object, its shadowy doppelgänger was bound to be lurking closely behind. From moment to moment, one would remain neutral in between the two energies. The eyes must be open, and one must see it for what it truly was: a battle.

The girl who sat silently next to the window was a part of who he had been, who he was, and the man he would become. There was a resilient connection between them which no blade could sever, and he had to find her because she signified all the beauty and purity he had always strived for. Her vision had haunted his dreams since he himself was a child.

The girl who sat by the window was his unborn daughter. She was his bid at immortality, and she was his motivation to fight toward the light. Cirrus had to do everything in his power to see beyond the darkness, because she was his own concealed piece of artwork. The pen in his shaky left hand had made first contact with a blank sheet of paper, giving life to his art. The time had come, and she had begun to materialize through him.

And new life was born.

Chapter One

It was strange for Cirrus Jacobs to see the walls in his apartment suite so bare and desolate. All that remained was a small mirror mounted on the wall facing east. From where he sat on the floor, he could see the reflection of a thin, aging man with short cropped hair staring back at him. The creases of age had appeared prematurely. What should've appeared as the face of a man in his mid-thirties had been weathered away to the heavy grooves of skin of a man in his late forties. It was an impossibility to transform the lines and curves on his face from an empty and expressionless one to one that might show even a hint of contentment. His eyes told it all.

Cirrus could hear the sound of dripping from the snow outside the window. He had lived in Vancouver his entire life, and the wet, grey weather never seemed to cease. Despite this, Cirrus loved his city, and it broke his heart knowing he'd have to leave it. Jacobs knew he needed a change, because for the last five years, it seemed the days had all been the same.

He'd wake up, go to work, exercise, and eat alone. This regimen was repeated over and over again. When he woke up next to the cold side of his bed, his heart ached. When he prepared the same chicken, rice, and vegetable entree day after day and sat eating alone in front of the television, he did it with a lump in his throat. As he watched the horrifying stories unfold on the news, the energy left his bones. His need to contribute to the world was so intense, yet he felt so utterly helpless.

After the second year of feeling this way, it had begun to show in his outward appearance. Upon a recommended visit from his boss, his doctor suggested that he take antidepressant drugs to inhibit selective serotonin levels in his brain. The diagnosis took all but seven minutes. Cirrus had willingly accepted the prescriptions and filled them every week for the last three years simply to get his boss off of his back. Jacobs didn't feel a pill should be so easily prescribed to offer artificial happiness, and since he couldn't stand the thought of passing poisons through his liver, he dutifully flushed them down the toilet every week.

Thinking, Cirrus closed his eyes. Surely, there had to be someone he could make happy, and someone to make him happy. There had to be more to life. There had to be something he could do to contribute. He had felt such a powerful hurt when he'd seen the images of Hurricane Katrina and 9/11 on his television screen, and he had wanted to help so badly. Yet, he didn't know where to begin. That was, of course, before he had decided to go searching for a path. Cirrus opened his eyes.

He sat silently, looking over his one-bedroom apartment. Even after he'd scrubbed down the walls several times with bleach, there remained the discoloration of the paint where he'd hung samples of his own photographic works. The traces left by the rectangular frames remained permanently imprinted on the walls like ghosts who refused to leave their homes. Jacobs had slept on the floor the night before because he had donated his bed, along with the rest of his belongings, to various charities three days before. He was never much for material possessions.

Cirrus felt he needed to stay there long enough to know it was absolutely the right time to embark on his journey, although he still had five days left on his rental agreement. The clothes he was wearing, a fresh change of clothes, some personal essentials, and a backpack to carry it all in were the only items he had chosen to keep. The only piece that really meant anything to him was an eight-foot-high bookshelf overflowing with books, which he had donated to the Vancouver Public Library.

If there was anything that fascinated Cirrus Jacobs in this world, it was the written word. An arrangement of a particular sequence of words, to form thoughts coherently, was one of humankind's greatest achievements. Weaving singular pearls together to make a full strand— it was a way of offering something to someone, even when one had nothing else tangible to give. The only other personal item he could not bear to part with was his camera.

When Cirrus was thirteen, he had earned money mowing lawns for the seniors in his neighbourhood that summer, and he ended up spending the bulk of his savings on that camera. He had originally intended to spend the money on a Christmas present for his grandmother, but his plans had changed along the way. Early in October he had been on his way to Sears to buy a new set of gardening tools for her when he passed by the storefront window of the pawnshop. During the twenty minutes he was in the store haggling the price down with the store clerk, the thoughts of his grandmother's Christmas gift vaporized out of his mind. It was the kind of amnesia only experienced by an excited child.

After realizing what he had done, he spent the entire forthcoming winter season shovelling snow from the sidewalks for the same old ladies for whom he had mown the lawns the previous summer. As a gesture to himself, perhaps as a means of justification, he took dozens of photographs of the cleared sidewalks with his new camera.

After seeing his grandmother's face when she opened up her present, he thanked God for the weeks of heavy snowfall they had received that year. It might've been the one and only time he'd thanked God for anything, as a matter of fact.

Seeing his grandmother kneeling in her vegetable patch, cultivating plants the following spring with the tools he had bought for her, was a memory that never faded for him.

He continued keeping up her garden for the three years he lived in that house after she had passed, but his thoughts would always return to her void in his life. Cirrus couldn't maintain it much longer after that. When he moved away, he made the new owners promise they would revitalize the garden again. He even gave them his grandmother's gardening tools as a housewarming gift. The husband couldn't have cared less, but the wife assured him that she would take care of the vegetable patch. He thought if he had the chance, he'd make his way over to the old house to visit; maybe he'd even pick up a few flowers for the wife to add to her garden.

Cirrus Jacobs suddenly found himself drifting away. Thinking about his grandmother always sent him into his imaginary world of

Paradoxum. He supposed it had always been his way of dealing with fear.

He knew that one step outside the door to his apartment was the beginning of a journey whose path he did not know, and whose outcome he could not predict. Cirrus couldn't help but feel a little uneasy. Inside his heart, he knew exactly where the final doorway stood, but at the time, it was something he tried not to think about.

Instead, he rose from his place on the floor and firmly placed two strong and heavy footsteps onto the hardwood surface and maintained a stance of valour, mostly to assure himself that he was strong enough to go through with his decision.

His sudden movement disturbed the still air and sent swirls of diminutive dust particles spiralling underfoot, exposing a once hidden beam of strong sunlight coming through the blinds. Knowing he had to get started with the day sooner or later, he quickly ran through his usual morning routine. After dressing in the same clothes he had slept in, he strapped on his backpack, picked up the box he had packed for John Everett down the hall, and pushed his key through the mail slot after locking up.

Cirrus set the package in front of John's door. He didn't bother knocking because he knew where John would be. Cirrus walked down the stairs and opened the lobby door, confirming his assumptions of Everett's whereabouts. He was sitting on the front stoop of their apartment complex drinking hot coffee from his thermos, as he did every morning. He didn't bother to look over his shoulder to see who he was talking to.

"Morning, Cirrus," Everett said.

Cirrus hadn't even uttered a single word. He supposed when people saw each other on a regular basis, they adapted to feeling each other's presence. Perhaps Cirrus emanated a distinct scent, or maybe the sounds of his footsteps had a recognizable pattern to them. Despite all this, nothing about John Everett ever surprised Cirrus. His intelligence, eyesight, hearing, and sense of smell were extremely acute. These were admirable qualities for anybody, but especially for a man in his seventies, as Mr. Everett was.

The steam rose from John's mug in thick ribbons, followed the contours of his chin and his face, and hovered momentarily at his

English cap before dissipating into the air. It sent a satisfying aroma of coffee along with it, and its smell heightened Jacobs's senses.

"Why don't you sit down and join me for a cup?" John said. "Somehow I knew we'd be running into each other this morning."

Cirrus peered though the coffee steam. "Mr. Everett, we run into each other every morning."

"Son, I've told you a million times to call me John. Addressing a man by calling him *mister* is how you would speak to an old man." At this, Cirrus squinted his eyes and offered a weak smirk.

All but the top four steps from the ground level were damp from the snow, and he took a seat on the third, one step below John. Everett carefully poured a cup for Cirrus in a small thermos mug. The coffee tasted even better than its aroma would dare to divulge, with just the right amount of Bailey's Irish Cream—to celebrate the holidays, of course.

Only a few clouds hung in the cold, brisk morning, clearing just enough to let the winter sun peek through. Its rays glistened through the foot of snow they'd received that week, sending reflections in every direction. Children could be heard playing in the distance. They pelted snowballs at each other, carefully built snowmen and igloos, and were bound on endless searches for makeshift hills in their suburban environment on which to test their new sleds. The sight of fresh snow never failed to remind Cirrus of those days he'd spent shovelling walkways for his grandmother, and her absence in his life made him ache.

John's deep voice resonated through the air when he spoke, billowing clouds of warm vapour into the cold air with each word. "Everything all right, son?"

Cirrus Jacobs turned his head toward the street. "Yeah," he said.

"Remember to breathe, that's all you need to know, son." John put an arm on Cirrus's shoulder, attempting to bear some of his weight.

"What does that mean?"

"It means exactly what I said. If you're smart enough, you'll figure that out one day," John replied with a raspy voice.

Cirrus contracted his brow and thought about this rather strange remark. He provided no response as they sat in silence, sipping their coffees and observing the scene. The voices of the children had begun to fade, and now they were barely a whisper; phantoms in the wind. They sat in silence, watching the cars drive by.

The day was beginning to unfold, as it should any Christmas morning. The neighbourhood began to fill with the smells of wood smoke from chimneys and roasting turkeys. People were plugging in their coloured Christmas lights and waving Merry Christmas greetings to each other in the streets. They sat, studying the still morning, and ultimately it was Cirrus who broke the silence. He had been rehearsing the dialogue in his head to phrase his sentence correctly. In the end, he just said it as simply as he could.

"John, I'm going away for a little while, I figured you should know. I don't want you to bring out an extra coffee cup for me anymore."

By the tone of his response, Cirrus could tell John wasn't surprised. "I know, Cirrus. I saw you hauling out your stuff earlier this week."

Cirrus continued anyway, like John hadn't said anything at all. "I haven't decided how long yet. I packed some stuff in a box for you and left it at your door. You can keep what's inside."

Cirrus knew John wouldn't ask what was in the box, so he'd let it be a surprise. Included were a few books and some old records he knew Everett would enjoy, and one other item he had expressed interest in when he came over from time to time. John and he would play chess on occasion, usually at John's apartment. The few times he knocked on Cirrus's door and they played at his place, a certain picture on the wall would always intrigue his eyes. Cirrus would constantly have to remind John it was his turn to move his piece, because he became fixated on the photograph. So, when he was assembling the package of items he would give to John, the last thing he included was a framed, black-and-white glossy of blues legend John Lee Hooker sipping espresso and smoking a cigar on a beautiful August afternoon. He had found it years earlier at a yard sale and bought it for fifty cents.

In the bottom of the box he'd left an old wristwatch his grandmother had given to him on his sixteenth birthday, which had once belonged to Cirrus's father. He didn't mention the watch to him because he knew John would refuse to take it. John Everett was the only person he could trust to take care of it for him, even though he'd never once been able to put it on his wrist.

"Where exactly are you going?" Everett asked.

"I don't really know, John," he said. "I have no one here, and I'm only telling you because you're the only one who'll notice I'm gone."

John didn't respond, but only looked into his coffee mug.

"I'm going on a walk, that's all I know," Jacobs said.

"What is it you're looking for, Cirrus?"

"I don't know for sure."

"Have you lost your mind, son?" John said with a smile.

Cirrus shrugged, afraid to make eye contact. "Don't know."

"Well, I've done some walking in my day, too, Cirrus. There's nothing you'll find out there that you can't find right here, son, that's a fact. Take it from an old man."

"I need to go anyway."

Cirrus had found himself at a loss for words. What was he supposed to say? That he had decided to leave his life and walk to some unknown destination? That the hurt inside of his chest was too much too bear? It sounded mad, even to him, and he didn't feel like explaining his instinct, so he remained silent.

"You'd better get going then, son," John said. "If you're going to be doing some traveling, then I suggest you follow the light for the short time it's around."

They had only been sitting a short time and his brisk send-off indicated that John surely had trouble with saying goodbye. Cirrus would admit, he did, too.

"Here, take my thermos with you."

The lump in Cirrus's throat prevented him from uttering any further parting words and he could only stand there with John's thermos clasped tightly in his hands. It wasn't until a few minutes had passed, that he finally built up the courage strong enough to walk down the front steps. He turned, but could not utter a single word.

"Go on now, son," Everett said.

Cirrus stood like an uncomfortable child for a few moments before finally making his way a few steps down the sidewalk. Silence was the only thing he could provide, as he bid his final farewell to John Everett.

"Remember to breathe and stay out of the cold," John said. "Time's wasting, son."

Before he turned and walked away, Cirrus used the camera in his knapsack to take a photograph of John. John watched Cirrus until he traveled far enough out of sight and then returned to his warm, morning coffee, as if nothing out of the ordinary had occurred.

He felt bad that he'd had to say goodbye to John Everett. An interesting man John was. Cirrus had the feeling John Everett was an occasional dweller of his own imaginary dream world. Cirrus supposed in some respects, everyone was. As he walked away, he wondered what John would have named his place of inner refuge. Would it have a name as strange as *Paradoxum*?

Cirrus walked without direction for several hours after that, not even bothering to look up to see where he was going. He simply let his instinct guide the path. Besides, he no longer cared where he was headed. If one were watching, Cirrus Jacobs seemed to be an ordinary man, walking the streets on a perfectly normal Christmas morning.

He didn't remember much of that first day, only that he walked hurriedly for hours upon end through the cold morning air. Behind him, walking relentlessly alongside his every step was a shadowy companion—his darkened twin, who identified himself only as Nimbus. Cirrus peered around through his peripheral vision but could not see him, yet felt his ominous presence, as always. He was there, yet remained as silent as a stalking panther. Cirrus sped his walk and distanced himself to avoid being prey. He closed his eyes to focus when he needed to, and continued walking.

* * *

Cirrus's first day was surreal and dreamlike. The time slipped by so fast that he could only recall bits and pieces of the events that occurred in his first twenty-four-hour period. Cirrus did recall that he walked for hours, brief memory fragments being burned during random moments.

After he parted company with Mr. Everett, he'd walked up and down the streets without looking up until he found himself edging his way closer towards the familiarity of the downtown core.

In the heart of downtown Vancouver, glorious buildings reached skyward between sporadic areas of lush greenery amid low-level housing complexes. The architecture encompassed all the magnificence of an utter masterpiece; every angle and stone face personifying the very labour of the people who built them, and he could almost see and feel them. To the north, there were mighty snow-capped mountains. An ocean lay to the west, branching dozens of arms of waterways through the landscape.

The closer he trod toward downtown, the more people littered the streets. He consciously avoided eye contact but was ambushed with cheery looks of holiday greetings nonetheless. Children, bundled from head to toe, were dragged along by their mothers; the fresh creases in their clothing suggesting brand new Christmas attire. Most of the shops and department stores were closed, but carols could be heard floating out of the few coffee houses that were still open. Although he'd been down those streets countless times, he felt as though it was his first time. In many ways, it was. There was a new freedom in his perception.

The wind began to pick up as he walked, scratching its freezing fingers alongside the back of his neck, plucking at his ears with its icy grip. One step after the other, he walked in a rhythmic pattern down the quiet streets of the city, sipping the coffee John had given to him as he trampled toward nothingness.

The buildings swept by his periphery in fast motion, a blur of store windows, address numbers, and neon signs. Cirrus's body blended into the concrete walkway, zigzagging around other pedestrians and mailboxes on the street. He walked with his head down, gazing only at his feet.

Left.

Right.

Left.

Right.

With each passing step he was becoming an incarnation of himself; he was one step further toward his destination.

Time was unconcerned with his doings and as the minutes ticked by, the air became colder and the once-blue sky now grew overcast with dark clouds. The everlasting battle between light and darkness resumed, as it did every day.

A short time ago it was clear and full of light, and now darkness began to move in, bringing with it what seemed to Cirrus to be heavy rain clouds. Still he walked, unaware of where he was going. Cirrus Jacobs walked steadily and without fatigue, making left and right turns on random, hopelessly wandering. The rhythm of his march helped to fade the minutes away.

As early evening approached, the first wave of bitter cold raindrops began to fall on his head. It ran through the strands of his hair, bulldozing rivers and creeks towards the ocean of his neck. Remembering John's advice to stay warm, Cirrus folded up the collar of his jacket to avoid losing any heat. He had subconsciously begun to shiver, and he wasn't sure if it was the temperature that caused the shuddering, or the fear that was slowly building up inside his chest. Cars sped by now and again, startling the hypnotic trance he was falling into. Surely they were panicked drivers racing to see which stores were still open, hoping to pick up some last minute ingredients for the night's feast. The hours passed as the rain fell, and he could already begin to feel the numbing of his memory. The truth was, it had begun months ago. Sometimes it seemed there weren't enough hours in a day, but this was not the case for Cirrus Jacobs. If there was no significance pinned to the events in a day, the hours could pass like bullets. He watched his feet ...

Left.

Right.

And so on.

His hypnotized march unwillingly led Jacobs into suburbia. It was a landscape where multicoloured flashing lights speckled every other house. Relaxing his pace, he carefully observed the scene. Chimney tops were swelling with dark smoke. Families could be seen laughing together with drinks in their hands, their silhouettes appearing segmented through the shuttered windows of their living rooms. There was less snow in that part of town and the ever-increasing rainfall had begun to melt the last of it away. Droplets of water were now pooled at the outermost edges of his brow, dripping every second as the hairs, which acted as reservoirs, became full to capacity. Cirrus's backpack and jacket were thoroughly drenched and the neckline of his shirt underneath was rapidly becoming a sponge as it absorbed the water that was running down his neck. Tendrils of steam lifted off of his clothes and hair in streams, cutting through the cold afternoon air. Still he walked forward.

He was shocked to look up and find that late afternoon was already beginning to metamorphosize into evening. He felt confused at how many hours he had lost walking with his head down. Now the rain seemed to fall stronger and colder. Its front line attackers were but a few sporadic drops, falling lightly from the sky. Now, they banded together in furious sheets, attempting to drown the streets. Puddles had now begun to form along the curbside and he fell victim to one of its assaults as a car drove by and launched the water into the air. It fanned his body with cold, dirty streams of water. Still he strode, further and further from all that was familiar. The emptiness in his body devoured all other senses, numbing even the coldness that shrouded him.

The streets all looked the same; it was the houses that began to change. As he strolled through the suburban landscape, it became quite evident where the line began to form that separated economic classes. The houses with brick faces and winding paving-stone walkways turned to concrete stucco and wood faces with cracked, asphalt paths. Some of them even had driveways strewn with gravel. The quality of cars began to subside, when eventually he walked into areas with only empty spaces where cars should have been parked. These houses were silent in comparison to the others; no families in the windows and no smoke coming out of the chimneys.

It was on these streets where he met his first road companion. Cirrus had noticed him a few blocks back following in silence, similar to a hunter scouting its prey. His dark brown fur hung down in thick mats from his sides and, much like Cirrus himself, he was completely soaked with water. This did not seem to bother the creature in the least, as he continued on his own path panting gently, streams of saliva stringing away from his exposed tongue. As Cirrus walked, his hearing remained acute. At first, he was unsure of its intentions. The blackness of fear began to swell inside of him until it displayed its lack of hostility by walking alongside Cirrus's footsteps, careful to stay at a safe distance. The sound of his wet paws touching the concrete was in the same rhythmic pattern as Cirrus's own footsteps. Because of his four walking limbs as opposed to Cirrus's two, its footsteps emanated twice as many beats. It was as if they played a jazz duet together; Cirrus played a solo on two strings of a slap bass, while the creature drilled out steady notes from a four-piece drum kit. It only walked with Cirrus for a short distance before deciding to disband and pursue a solo career, scurrying off into the darkness of the night.

Although hidden, and taking the more exploratory route, it didn't stray far. He surfaced from the shadows now and again, sometimes choosing to walk on Cirrus's side of the street, sometimes on the other, and sometimes even in the middle of the street. In his mind, Cirrus pretended that it was his pet dog, with a name like Jake or Gus, and he walked him through the streets unleashed. They'd take a quick walk through the neighbourhood together before going back to the house and joining the family for Christmas dinner. These ridiculous thoughts occupied his mind as he walked, watching his feet …

Left.

Right.

And so forth.

Cirrus looked up to see the dog's silhouette about a hundred feet ahead, through the silver lines of rainfall and barely visible in the streetlight. It seemed he had run a distance ahead, and was now sitting obediently on the sidewalk waiting for Cirrus to catch up. His eyes captured the last remaining particles of early evening light and reflected them back to Cirrus. The look in them told Cirrus that he knew it was not the case between them. Cirrus knew as well as the dog did, that they were both stray creatures. There was no blazing fireplace, hot dinner, or loving family to welcome them home. In reality, the coming darkness was the only thing waiting out for them on that cold Christmas night. The dog knew this very well, and so did Cirrus.

The dog waited until he came within reach before electing himself leader, and continuing the path. They walked together for over three hours through the densely populated suburbs until the houses began to fade and the dark streets eventually wound their way toward a park. The distance closed enough to use the streetlights to see. He saw an old wooden sign that read "Queen's Park." Cirrus noticed that virtually every surface was covered in graffiti; the play area and monkey bars were the most abused victims. As if that were not enough, his steps needed to be carefully orchestrated to avoid walking over the garbage and dog shit that covered the grass like leftover landmines.

The dog, whom Cirrus had now named Jake, ran ahead to make his own contribution and relieved himself on a tree. Cirrus took a seat on a bench halfway into the park, soaking up the rain. Now that he had sat down after walking constantly throughout the entire day, his feet began to ache. They pulsated in his shoes while shivers possessed the rest of his body. Subconsciously, he curled up sideways on the bench to compact and conserve some heat. His new friend had also found himself a spot to rest alongside the trunk of a massive fir tree, protected by its enormous wingspan of branches. Jake the dog kept his ears on things, twitching whenever a car door slammed or a voice cried out in the distance.

Strange as it seemed, Cirrus felt quite comfortable there using the darkness of the night as a blanket. Although his watch read only 6:30 pm, he had now begun to feel overwhelmed with weariness. Before he fell asleep entirely, he sat upright and took a photograph of Jake the dog. The dog provided no reaction, as if he had been a professional model for many years. Lying with his head resting on his paws, his body gently rocked back and forth, panting out the troubles of his day. Cirrus resumed his position on the bench as his eyes become heavier until inevitably he gave up resistance and succumbed to the darkness that resided inside the inner walls of his eyelids. The eerie silence was their only other companion in the night. The image of Jake the dog was the last he'd see in the night before his sleep transferred him into the dream world of Paradoxum.

*　　*　　*

In the confines of reality, Cirrus Jacobs was huddled on a bench attempting to conserve his body heat, in a park on an unnamed street, amid the ever-fading daylight. In his imaginary world of Paradoxum, he was running. From what, he didn't know, but always running. The dream world of Paradoxum was not always filled with the tender images of the life he'd wished he could have; it was quite often the opposite. This was the darkness that was always on his trail, the *shadow,* if you will. Most would define these images as mere nightmares, but Cirrus knew better; he knew it was more. This was the battle that raged on day after day.

His dreams were always void of much detail, only enough to know he didn't want to be engulfed in them; his instinct told him that much. As he ran through a labyrinth of stygian paths and walls, he searched for *her*. Painted of black stone and dirty corners, the paths branched into boundless directions, as if alive. With the dark mist at each footstep, his lungs heaved rapidly in his chest, knowing that his oxygen must not be wasted on screams.

What were these entities that pursued Cirrus Jacobs so relentlessly? Were they perhaps demons of conscience and guilt? Were they purveyors of uncertainty and fear? He didn't know for sure, and it only contributed further to his confusion. He had merely found this place, not created it. It was part of the constant hurt that he felt. He always ran as fast as he could until he could run no farther. And that was where it always ended, at the edge. Although these descriptions were rather cryptic, he could explain them no other way. Trying to explain a strange dream to someone into a tangible recreation was an utter impossibility. It was more an experience rather than a narrative.

A voice interrupted … *his* voice. It hissed through the mist. "Wake up, Cirrus."

"Who's there?"

"Must we go through this again?" the voice said. Cirrus clenched his fists.

"It is I, Nimbus. And it is you who has given me this name. How quickly we forget."

At that moment, the reality of the world snapped back as quickly as it had come. It had seemed as if months had passed. Cirrus awoke with a jerk of his muscles, still panting heavily.

His eyes began to clear and his mind immediately started looking for evidence of recognition in his surroundings. The clarity came slowly, and it occurred to Cirrus that he was back in the confines of the waking world. He heard only the sound of rain, no voices.

Jake was nowhere to be found; perhaps he went searching through the neighbourhood garbage cans for some food. The world was now negated of colour altogether, and the only illumination in the night sky was the glow of the moon. Far in the distance, street posts and Christmas lights showed the way and it was in their vagueness that Cirrus searched for a glimpse of his canine friend, but to no avail. The shivering in his body had subsided temporarily although the rain fell steadily, cold and unrelenting. He sat on the bench soaking up the rain in silence, although for some inexplicable reason he felt like screaming at the top of his lungs. It seemed his image resting beneath the tree would be the last Cirrus would see of old Jake the dog.

Hesitantly, he once again allowed his feet to choose their own direction, heading away from Queen's Park. The downtown lights of the horizon far in the distance produced a strange effect on the layers of the backdrop of clouds. It was a terrifying optical illusion. The hum of the city lights appeared as a vicious fire radiating along the ground, twisting the shadows of the clouds above unto themselves. The clouds resembled thick billows of dark smoke scattered across the sky, escaping from the blazing inferno of the burning city. An optical illusion that lasted a fraction of a second; and strangely enough, it was in this direction his feet chose to walk.

The moon was hidden away, but its incandescence could be seen behind the ominous clouds. Pure white light beneath the mist, offering its presence as a substitution for Jake the dog as an unspoken friend. As he continued to walk toward the downtown streets, his stomach began to cry. Perhaps triggered by the smells of roasting turkey in the air, it let out deep growls of attention, which he ignored. His mind was caught in a whirlwind of time from which he could not escape, and hunger had no place there. He had been preparing himself mentally for months and had been slowly conditioning himself to abandon the concept of time, only allowing himself to focus on the rhythm of his feet. Left and right were the only two things that concerned him now.

He walked toward the light of the city until commercial buildings began to replace the houses. On the concrete sidewalks and within the whirlwind of his mind he walked, sacrificing his body to the instinct. It mattered little if he'd been walking in circles, he hadn't decided on a clear direction to his destination anyway. The streets felt extremely dark and menacing. The trees which lined the streets curled toward the sidewalks on which he walked, like giant claws closing in on a small rodent. Cirrus had no other choice than to concentrate on the rhythm and walk toward the lights of the city, his body shaking with these thoughts. He didn't know exactly how many hours had passed since he'd left the park. Hypnosis from his steps began to consume him until from out of the silence her voice broke his trance.

"Good evening, sir."

He stopped to look up and attempted to focus, trying to push back the vertigo that swelled inside his brain. A cigarette dangled between her fingers as she exhaled deep smoke with her sentence, speaking with a slightly hoarse voice. Her plump body was merely a silhouette beneath the brightly lit sign that read: "Ray of Light," casting shadows over the contours of her face. Cirrus reached his hand out to block the light and struggled to gain focus. The words *Ray of Light* piqued his curiosity. He knew to keep his eyes open for any progress toward the place he was seeking.

She repeated herself. "Good evening." After some hesitation, she continued. "Are you all right, sir?"

"I'm fine," he answered. "I've just been walking all day and I suppose I wasn't paying attention to where I was going, that's all."

"What are you doing walking around at this hour on Christmas day? Have you got no place to go?"

He nodded his head in response, ashamed to answer her question. She flicked the remaining part of her cigarette onto the street, where it rolled into the gutter, and stepped forward with her hand extended. "I'm Judith Edgewater."

"Cirrus Jacobs, pleased to meet you, Ms. Edgewater."

"Cirrus?" she asked. "That's an unusual name, isn't it?"

"I suppose."

"Cirrus, like the clouds?"

"Yes, ma'am, like the clouds," he said.

"The wispy type, like the kind you might see at sunset, those the ones?"

He forced a weak smile. "Yes."

"Well, pleased to meet you, too, Cirrus," she responded, looking satisfied that she knew the meaning of his name. As she stepped back under the lights of the sign, her scent filled his nose. It was a strange odour, a subtle floral perfume mixed with the smells of food which emanated from her apron. Rain dripped from his hair onto his shoes, spraying tiny bits of water onto her shoes as well. She reached out and grabbed his cold hands, pulling him toward her with a jerk underneath the protection of the awning.

"Look at you, son, you're completely soaked with water. If you're not careful, you'll catch pneumonia." She sounded like Mr. Everett to him, always worried about the weather. He didn't even think pneumonia was still considered a threat.

"If you're hungry, you're more than welcome to join us inside for dinner, there's plenty of food left." With her dialogue, she opened the front door of the shelter, exposing dozens of people sitting at tables eating a charitable version of a Christmas dinner. The aroma of the food tantalized all five of his senses, causing his mouth to salivate. So much for conditioning and discipline, he thought.

The people who sat at the tables were obviously without homes, and had wandered in out of the cold, much like Cirrus himself. One of them caught his eye through the open doorway and immediately looked down into his plate when Jacobs acknowledged his observations. While the others talked among themselves, this one was left alone, sitting by himself. His dark beard showed signs of greying and his face was streaked with heavy creases of age.

Ms. Edgewater held the door open while she patiently waited for Cirrus to make a decision, looking out into the rainy streets. After smelling the food that she offered, the hunger impulse in his stomach was now too strong to ignore; besides, he'd need somewhere to dry off.

Cirrus kept his voice low and humble. "Thanks. I'll help with some duties around the kitchen in exchange for a meal. How does that sound?"

"Deal," she replied with a smile, still gazing out into the streets. She moved aside enough to let him pass. As he took the first step in, the faces looked up to catch sight of the newcomer. A dozen pairs of eyes focused their attention on Cirrus through tensed brows, and he could feel their gaze. Several young children sat next to their mothers, eating quietly. The room smelled like dirty, rain-soaked clothing and the heating system only helped to strengthen the mildewed odour, sending thick wafts of pungent smells into the air. The eyes looked away and the silence ceased to exist after a few moments as they became less interested in him and returned to their previous conversations.

A long, narrow table was set up in the far corner of the room in front of the kitchen entrance, and the sound of pots and pans could be heard over the noises of the crowd. Two young students volunteered their services at either ends of the table, scooping out food to the hungry people in line.

"Go on now, Cirrus, have yourself a plate," Judith said as she brushed past him and hurried into the kitchen. One of the students, a young girl with shoulder-length blonde hair, stood at the front of the line serving food, her hair tied expertly in a ponytail. She armed herself with a pair of tongs in one hand and a serving spoon in the other, carefully and kindly placing the portions of food onto the plates as people moved by. Several more bodies began to come in out of the cold and the volume of conversation quickly doubled, bringing with it a cold howl of the wind each time the door opened.

"Merry Christmas," she said as he moved up in the line, his plate fully extended. Her energy and eagerness to help others was quite evident in the gentle tone of her voice. Somehow her kind demeanour felt familiar. Perhaps it was his grandmother that her kindness reminded him of.

"My name is Cirrus," he responded quietly. "Thank you."

She served a generous portion of turkey with one hand, and a heaping scoop of mashed potatoes with the other. "You're welcome."

Cirrus offered a smile in gratitude as he continued to move down the line, observing from the conversation behind him that not everyone was as patient or polite as he was trying to be. He had only been out for a single night without food and shelter and was already beginning to feel the effects from the elements. Who knew for how long some of the others had starved? He supposed they had a right to be impatient, even if that meant being inadvertently rude. Still, she greeted every person with a warm holiday greeting, regardless if they responded with friendliness or not; it was obvious her actions were born of pure unselfishness. Cirrus turned back as he reached the end of the line when her eyes met his, and they seemed to share some kind of connection. Through silence, he tried to relay his gratefulness once again. In her eyes, he saw the same qualities that resided in Mr. Everett's, the same he saw in his own reflection. The spark of the *searcher*. It was a quality possessed by those who visited their own dream worlds, without a doubt.

His plate was overflowing with food as he turned to overlook the room to find a seat among the tables. There were several left, but his eyes were drawn to the table where the old man sat. He remained silent, eating slowly. The same man who was looking through the open doorway when Cirrus came in, now sat gazing into nothingness, his eyes strangely unfocused. The clothes on his back were tattered and dirty, and they clung to his body in sheets of fabric from the rain. His shoes were darkened and torn, and the soles were withered completely away. He sat like a ghost among the living, slowly chewing his food, and the others paid him no attention. He didn't stir an inch or make an attempt at eye contact when Cirrus took a seat directly in front of him.

"Hello, my name is Cirrus."

The chair squeaked noisily as Cirrus sat down and adjusted his seat, which also failed to catch the old man's attention. Cirrus supposed that if he'd wanted to talk, he'd have initiated the conversation himself. For the remainder of his meal, Cirrus maintained silence. He'd finished his plate within ten minutes, and in that entire time, the old man hadn't uttered a single sound. Jacobs's thoughts would repeatedly return to the shoes on the man's feet, as he picked at the remaining vegetables on his plate. The food, which didn't look very appetizing at first, turned out to be quite enjoyable, although Cirrus would be the first to admit he was quite hungry.

Immediately after clearing away the last morsel off his plate, Cirrus stood up and offered yet another introduction, hoping the old man might talk now that he'd had some food in his belly. He leaned forward and whispered his words. "It was nice having Christmas dinner with you."

The old man continued eating his food without a response, chewing heartily at his mashed potatoes. The white fluff took up about ninety percent of his entire plate, with little room left over for equal amounts of turkey, stuffing, and vegetables. Everything was thoroughly doused with dark gravy. Convinced that he didn't want to speak, Cirrus stood and turned to return his dishes when the old man's eyes turned from his plate. They were deep brown with a misty opaqueness that covered each iris, indicating the possibility of a mild cataracts condition. At Cirrus's smile, the old man returned his gaze to the food and continued eating as if he had momentarily spotted an old friend, and realized he had been mistaken.

Jacobs walked across the room and the student at the chow line pointed him toward the kitchen, where he found Ms. Edgewater basting the last of the roasting turkeys.

"Where can I start, Ms. Edgewater?" he asked.

"Have you had enough to eat, son?"

"Yes, ma'am, I have," he said. "What can I do to help out?"

"You can start by giving me your backpack and your jacket. I'll set them aside to dry." She looked over the countertops. His gaze followed. "See that man over there?" she said. "That's Roy, he's in charge. He'll show you what needs to be done and you can find an apron in the storeroom. Good?"

Cirrus did as she asked, handing over his belongings and retrieving an apron. Roy worked at the far end of the kitchen, concentrated on his work, completely oblivious to Cirrus's presence in the kitchen. Roy's thick hands grated steaming Idaho potatoes through a ricer as he added an array of spices into the creation without any measurement. The dark shadow of hair could be seen beneath his hairnet, showing a shiny bald scalp at the top. Cirrus assumed from the spotlessness of Roy's apron, that he was a pro at what he did, meticulous in every detail. His eyes didn't leave his work as Cirrus spoke.

"Roy?"

Roy's voice was a deep, hoarse rumble. "What is it?" Its resonance sent shivers up Cirrus's spine.

"My name is Cirrus Jacobs. I'm here to give you a hand."

Roy's massive frame and callous demeanour overshadowed the entire room, casting everything else in the room into insignificance. It was like a single voice trying to be heard among a concert full of thousands. Still, Roy's eyes remained fixated on the heaping mound of mashed potatoes. "There are two bags of carrots in the cooler. Grab a bin and start peeling, when you're done with those, start on more potatoes—we serve meals every day, not just today. Any questions?"

"No, sir," Cirrus said. He wasn't about to talk to this man any more than he needed to. In the cooler, Cirrus found the carrots and quickly set up an area to work on the countertop. Rhythm was everything and it was with this tool that Cirrus did his work. Similar to the pulse he concentrated on when he'd been walking, as so he peeled the carrots. Strangely, there was nothing else on his mind. For the first time in a long while the drone in his mind had taken a rest and, for the time being, Nimbus seemed to be in slumber.

Roy and Ms. Edgewater were focused on their own work as the low hum of a small clock radio whispered out classical arrangements from the local station. Cirrus let the sounds of the radio float into his head as he worked.

He toiled through two bags of carrots and continued with the potatoes until Ms. Edgewater walked over and told him to join her in the dining room when he was finished with the last box. Cirrus placed the last of the six buckets, which were filled with peeled potatoes and cold water, into the cooler and washed up. Roy had long since gone home. Along with Ms. Edgewater, the student with the blonde hair was the only other person left in the shelter. It seemed as Cirrus was working, the last of the diners had left.

As he walked out of the kitchen, he found them sitting together, quietly sipping hot liquid from their mugs.

Ms. Edgewater stood and slid over a chair. "Sit down. How about some hot chocolate?"

He forced a smile again. "I'd love some." She briskly made for the kitchen as he took a seat next to the student. "I wanted to say thanks again for dinner."

"No problem," the girl said. "You're Cirrus, right?"

"Yeah."

Her eyes squinted as she smiled, nervously adjusting her mug. "I'm Tara."

Ms. Edgewater came walking back in the room with a steaming cup in one hand and his belongings in the other. She placed the backpack on the floor and hung his jacket on the back of her chair. "Wait here one minute," she ordered.

She left the room again with Tara and Cirrus staring past each other's shoulders in silence, trying awkwardly to find some suitable conversation. In the adjacent room, shuffling noises could be heard as they drank their hot chocolates without a word.

After a few minutes, Judith returned to their table. "Here, take these."

In her hand she held a yellow rubber raincoat and a matching hat. They were quite obviously worn, but still looked to be functional. Just as Cirrus was about to decline her offer, she interjected. "Don't say no, Cirrus, just take them. Somebody has to put them to use."

Cirrus took the jacket and held it up to his chest. Surprisingly, it looked to be a perfect fit. "Thank you very much," he said after a pause. "For everything, Ms. Edgewater."

She took a seat and looked across the table toward the window. "Call me Judith."

The rain had turned to snow and in the short time he was in the kitchen, it had laid a three-inch blanket over the city. As he looked toward the sky, he noticed it falling quite thickly and steadily. Snow had a peculiar way of absorbing the sounds outside, and this phenomenon amplified even the slightest noises inside the room. He could clearly hear the three of them breathing.

Judith interrupted the short moment of silence as she stood. "I'm going to step out for a cigarette."

Judith took their soundlessness as permission and walked out the front door after putting on her coat and hat. As the glass door opened, a vicious billow of cold wind pushed its way into the room. Cirrus placed his hands around the hot mug to keep his fingers warm. Tara put her hands around her elbows and bunched herself close together, mimicking an implosion of the body. Judith, on the other hand, looked quite warm and comfortable through the open blinds, lighting her cigarette.

The bright lights cast a spotlight above her head and over her body, darkening the images behind her, and made her look angelic in a strange sort of way. The thought of an angel deeply inhaling a cigarette brought a smile to Cirrus's face.

It was just the irony of it, that's all.

Chapter Two

The sound of the baby crying in the next room awakened Raymond, as it did every morning. He was quite used to it by then; besides, he enjoyed waking up to the sounds of his daughter. He had always been a light sleeper, unlike Emily, who almost always slept right through the morning noises. The sun shone its brilliance behind the drawn curtains and slightly began to heat up the room. It had been a moderately warm winter with only a few short days of snow that season, although Raymond had been hoping for his daughter's first holiday to be a white Christmas. It was certainly strange weather that year for Montreal.

She whimpered quietly in her crib in the adjacent room, which Raymond had converted from a home office to a nursery. Little Julia Porter never cried too loudly; partly because she wasn't fussy, and partly because she hadn't quite possessed the lung capacity yet. Raymond pulled aside the covers and sluggishly picked himself out of bed. He looked over his wife as she slept, memorizing her every detail at that moment. The locks of her tightly spiralled hair were strewn over the pillow like the fan of a peacock's feathers, exposing the softness of her face. To Raymond, it was clearly one of the wonders of the world how she still managed to look so captivating, even as she slept.

He walked over to the window and slid the curtains aside, careful not to make any unnecessary noises and disturb his girls. The day was filled with sunshine, as it had been for the last few days. Its rays brought colour to the landscape, intensifying their already blinding richness. He walked out of the room and entered the nursery where his daughter Julia slept. She had already stopped crying, adhering to the rules of their morning ritual. Somehow, she sensed her father's presence and patiently waited for him to come to her.

Raymond stood in the doorway with his arms crossed, leaned against the frame, and gazed upon his daughter. He could see Julia's arms flailing wildly just over the top of the crib's wooden prison bars. She reached for the mobile, fascinated by its dazzling array of colours, trying to persuade her dad to turn on its musical wonders.

He leaned forward and whispered, "Hey, baby."

The sound of his unmistakable voice made her excitement grow beyond control and she made an attempt at communication, only able to produce a few muffled infant grunts. Ray walked over and gently picked up his child, supporting the back of her neck with the palm of his right hand, which in comparison was colossus. Her hair had begun to grow in thicker now and he hoped perhaps she'd grow to have rich curls like her mother.

Raymond Porter walked through the house with Julia nestled on his chest, humming the random tune he woke up with in his head that morning. She silently enjoyed his effort, not yet able to realize just how off-key he actually was. He circled the halls once and entered the room where his wife still slept, crouching near the edge of the bed and leaning closer. He gave her a soft kiss on the forehead.

"Ray?" she asked.

"I'm here."

"What time is it?"

"Just before eight," he said. Emily kept her eyes closed, afraid to let in the piercing rays of the morning sun. He absorbed the warmth of her soft skin as he kissed her forehead for a second time. "Here, take Julia," he said. "I'm going to start the coffee."

Emily pushed aside the covers with her eyes still sealed shut, and arranged the blankets in a nest against her body for the baby. With the knowledge of his two girls safely sleeping in their bedroom, Raymond walked into the kitchen to begin his day.

After the machine began its brewing cycle, he opened the front door of his house to retrieve the morning paper. Despite the fact that Ray had repeatedly told the delivery boy to make sure the paper was tossed all the way to the doorstep, his aim was never accurate. Every morning without fail, the paper would be resting at the bottom of the steps. Ray didn't really mind though; it had become part of his morning routine along with his daughter's wake-up service. He decided to leave it be until his hand was holding a steaming cup of coffee, at which point he returned to the front porch and took a seat outside with the paper unfolded on the tabletop. As Raymond sat in the wicker patio chair, the wind chimes that were bolted to the front support beam rang a soft tune in response to the morning breeze.

Most of the cars in the neighbourhood were parked in their driveways because their owners were still in the midst of their Christmas holidays. Birds chirped loudly as they flew in and out of the evergreen tree in front of Raymond and Emily Porter's home. She had fastened a bird feeder onto a branch about a quarter-length up the tree last spring, and since then, the word had gotten out among the feathered community. Ray observed them with a smile as he read the morning paper.

His eyes scanned the pages uninterestedly for several moments until a headline caught his attention: *Homeless Man Perishes in Below-Freezing Temperatures on West Coast.*

Like most people, Raymond had progressively become numb to most of the cynical headlines he came across in the daily newspaper because most of them read the same every day. It was precisely this type of story that helped to keep him from becoming indifferent altogether, whether he recognized it at all. Unable to conceal the sympathy he felt at this senseless tragedy, he tried in honesty to commemorate the nameless and faceless man who had died alone in the cold. He also thanked God for the life he had been privileged enough to have, and for his wife and child.

This internal event happened briefly, until a voice broke him out of this momentary train of thought. "Ray?"

She stood in the doorway wearing only one of his blue dress shirts, and the slippers he had put in her stocking for Christmas. Her face was without makeup and the features of her natural beauty dimmed even the beams of sunlight that fell from the sky. This had been one of the characteristics that had first attracted Raymond to her so many years ago. He glanced up from his newspaper and automatically smiled at her presence—at her perfection.

"What were you frowning at?" she said.

"Something I read in the paper."

31

"What was it?" she insisted.

Instead of answering, Ray neatly folded his paper and walked over to her. He wrapped his arms around Emily's waist and placed a gentle kiss on the back of her neck. She closed her eyes and smiled as she received his affection and they walked into the kitchen to join their daughter, who was waiting patiently in her high chair for a meal of puréed something or other.

Raymond Porter helped his wife clean the kitchen after breakfast and then joined her in the living room while Julia quietly looked on from her playpen. The room was scattered with boxes and packing material as Ray and Emily carefully wrapped glassware from the center of the cardboard fortress.

"Are you getting excited about the move?" he asked.

"It is getting close, isn't it?"

"Only a few more days," he responded. "How is your mother taking it?"

"She still thinks you could find an equal job right here in town, but I suppose she's getting used to the idea of us moving away."

"Emily, we've been through this," he said. "Besides, there's less than a week to go."

"I know, she's just going to miss us, that's all."

"Once we get settled in, she can fly out to visit any time she wants."

Emily looked to the window and said, "I know."

She quietly remained wrapping the glassware with newspaper as Ray began to dismantle the artificial Christmas tree and box away the decorations. He had wanted a real tree for his daughter to experience, but with all that was going on with the move, they opted for a two-foot imitation evergreen. They had both agreed to a small holiday celebration that year and the tree stood as a symbolic reminder of this decision. Three months ago, Raymond had received a job offer with the west coast branch of his investment firm, and six weeks after that, he had accepted.

The move would undoubtedly be toughest for Emily, whose entire family lived there. She had a small handful of friends in the city, most of whom she hadn't seen since she graduated college four years prior. Raymond had discussed the matter with his wife every day for a full three weeks until they decided it was best for the financial future of their family. Raymond didn't exactly like the idea of their daughter growing up in such a big city, but in the end, determined it might be a learning experience for all of them. His contract to the company only committed them for three years in the city and they would be free to return home if they wanted after that. As it happened to be, this turned out to be the major contributing factor to their verdict.

"Did you check the weather forecast for next week?" Emily asked.

Getting frustrated, Ray answered over his shoulder as he haphazardly crammed the Christmas tree branches into the tiny box, which did not seem to be fitting. "Yes, possible snow flurries, but mostly rain. Typical Vancouver."

"What about the highways, how are they?"

He tried not to sound annoyed at his wife's line of questioning, even though her inquiries in conjunction with the tree were beginning to aggravate him. "I don't know, Emily." He was never one to lose his cool, especially around his wife whom he would go to great lengths not to offend.

"Just don't forget to pack the tire chains," she said. "We don't want to get caught in the snow without them."

"Okay, Em," he muttered under his breath, still wrestling with the tree.

She began to pick up on her husband's irritation and decided to change the subject. Emily Porter could always sense when Raymond became exasperated with a certain topic and knew when to change the direction of the conversation. She appreciated his patience and serene demeanour; in fact, it was one of her favourite qualities about him. Despite their avoidance with each other during certain conversations, there was rarely an opportunity given for the possibility that their communication might begin to deteriorate. Emily and Ray Porter connected on a different plane, as he liked to think. On some level he could not explain, perhaps in another world, perhaps in another dimension. The reverence and adoration they held for each other came from the trust and strength in their communication, binding them together like the thick, woven fibres of a rope.

Seconds before Raymond let his frustration get the better of him, and entertaining the idea of throwing the tree through the window, the last of the branches fit neatly into the box. He turned wide-eyed and red-faced to his wife, who was desperately trying to control her hysterics. Together, they broke into a roar of laughter, and all that might've been building into a potential argument disintegrated. Julia smiled as she played in her playpen, unaware of the actions taking place. Her only interest was the harmonious sound of laughter coming from her parents.

As Raymond, Emily, and little Julia Porter made preparations for their move, an opposite existence continued to unfold in the city they were destined for.

Without their knowledge, a man they had yet to meet named Cirrus Jacobs awakened from his first night as a homeless man.

Chapter Three

Cirrus Jacobs awakened the next morning convinced that Ms. Judith Edgewater had saved his life the night before. If it hadn't been for the raingear, he would have either drowned or frozen to death. The night had been filled with freezing rain and wet snow, continuing on throughout the morning. He hadn't really slept much the night before, although he tried as hard as he could. It was still very early, only five o'clock, and the darkness had yet to be lifted.

He parted company with Judith and Tara as soon as he'd finished his hot chocolate. By the time Judith had finished smoking her cigarette, he had started to become uneasy. Unexplainable nervousness began to build up inside his chest. Perhaps it was the uncertainty of spending the night without a roof over his head or perhaps *Nimbus* had awakened. They seemed a little surprised at his eagerness to return to the cold streets, but he'd desperately felt a need to be alone. Cirrus needed to find somewhere to pass the hours of the night away.

Before leaving, he had handed a hundred-dollar bill to Judith to add to the shelter's contribution box. She was taken aback at first with his charity, but Cirrus convinced her to take the money. Unknown to her, the wallet in his back pocket still contained over three thousand dollars in cash. He had obtained it by closing his savings account at the bank and selling the beaten-up old car he used to travel back and forth from work. The truth was he didn't even know why he possessed the money at all; he had no real use for it. Before Cirrus Jacobs walked away from his job, his apartment, and his life, he wasn't sure how things were going to be. It had always been his nature to have preparations set aside and he supposed he had the money as a safety net of sorts. Regardless, it felt good to give it away. Maybe he'd get rid of it all.

He had asked Ms. Edgewater to spend some of it on a new pair of shoes for the bearded old man that was eating at the shelter. Cirrus couldn't keep his thoughts from repeatedly returning to the worn shoes on the old man's feet; broken and dirty, like the man himself. As he said goodbye, she sent him off with a thin blanket, which he had carefully folded and stored inside his backpack. Judith had also told Cirrus that she and Roy could use extra help in the kitchen whenever he felt like coming in.

Cirrus supposed his thoughts of the old man were recurring because of those shoes. The decrepit condition of his footwear suggested that he spent a great deal of time walking. It scared him a little because he saw himself in the old man. What he had become might very well personify Cirrus's own possible future, although he hoped there was an end somewhere in sight for his destination.

Cirrus's path to Paradoxum was going to be a long one, and part—if not all—of the traveling had to be done by foot. He wasn't merely searching for a palpable location, but for verification that Paradoxum existed at all. It was enlightenment that Cirrus hoped to find in his journeys, or some kind of constant truth anyway. He supposed it didn't really matter what names he gave these places, just some evidence that light and purity actually did exist.

Cirrus fully understood that there may have been an impending state of derangement lurking inside his mind, but he was still painfully aware of the sanity that he still possessed, and being sentient of his own mind state was lucidity in itself. He was afraid if the darkness overpowered the light, his sanity might vanish forever, and this was the cause of his constant fear. His loneliness and isolation had begun to get the better of him. It weighed on his shoulders like bags of concrete—that, and the fact he was occasionally visited by a strange voice inside his head who called himself Nimbus. Cirrus needed to know and see for himself why life truly was a precious and valuable force, and why he had to fight to hold on to it.

Looking up at the darkened sky, Cirrus Jacobs let the snowflakes wash over his face. The heat from his skin melted them on contact, and he opened his mouth to quench his thirst. The icy droplets felt fresh and provided him with a sense of being cleansed. The night before, he had returned to the same park he had rested at with Jake the dog. The soaring trees and resulting seclusion provided the cover that he needed to make it through the night. He was as awake then as he was when he'd left Mr. Everett less than twenty-four hours before; although to him, that already felt like a lifetime away. Jake the dog never returned, as he'd been hoping. There were a few times during the night when he'd heard the barking of dogs, but their yelps never matched the strange implication of freedom he found in Jake's.

Jacobs's thoughts remained in a whirlwind as he watched the snow fall from above, shimmering in front of the lonely glow of the streetlights. A few dry flakes had managed to integrate themselves in, crystallizing on the treetops. His body was covered with water from head to toe on the exterior, but thanks to Ms. Edgewater, the clothes inside were dry and warm. Despite the body heat he generated, his muscles shivered beneath the rubber raingear. He lay there in a fetal position on a wooden bench, afraid to close his eyes. Surely the park would be filled with children playing in the snow come morning, and he was equally terrified of encountering Nimbus as he was of waking up to a group of people pointing fingers in the daylight. The low hum of the wind rustled his clothing and sent throbbing electricity pulses through his brain. He had made the mistake of sitting still for several hours, and now his muscles had developed a slight atrophy from the cold.

He had to keep moving.

Once again, he walked toward the lights of the downtown buildings. Lucky for him, the streets didn't seem nearly as intimidating the second time around. Cirrus's hearing was held at high alert in the hopes he'd hear the four-step trot of Jake. Instead, his own footsteps were the only ones he heard.

Left and right: it had now become his own personal mantra. He could feel the beating of his heart as he inhaled the cold air and processed it out as warm vapor. Leaning forward and letting his legs absorb the momentum, this action drove him forward.

His thoughts were still with the old man. Cirrus had imagined himself with a long beard and torn sneakers walking down the streets, uttering unintelligible phrases into the wind. He wondered what events had led up to this man's present state. Was there anyone on earth who still remembered his name? Would he be missed when he was gone?

Cirrus's stomach rumbled loudly as he walked, as if voicing its opinion on the matter. He had made his way into the city faster than the night before; perhaps it was his hunger that pushed him closer. The sky was still very dark and the wet snow continued to cover the city. Near emptiness filled the buildings, and as he sauntered further into the heart of the metropolis, lights began to illuminate some of the restaurants and coffee shops as they opened for breakfast.

There were a few people scattered about, those not fortunate enough to have the day after Christmas as a day off. He walked by the storefront window of a small café and met eyes with a young lady who was refilling the sugar and cream containers on the tables inside. She was of possible Caribbean descent, and her hair was pulled back in tight braids. Her skin was of the same natural color of the coffee beans brewing behind the counter. She smiled at him, exposing a perfect set of glossy teeth. He smiled back, unable to deflect her positive brilliance. The moment lasted only seconds as he passed by.

Left. Right. Left: his sidewalk hypnosis resumed.

Walking through the slush had caused his socks to become completely sodden with water and the sound of the swishes accompanied the sounds of his soles hitting the concrete. The roars from his stomach were gradually growing in frequency like labor contractions.

He ducked into the first fast-food restaurant he came across, and swung open the heavy glass doors to find a nearly empty seating area. The smell of bacon and eggs was strong and the heat produced by the grill hung in the air. Its collision with his frigid skin produced a tingling sensation and his nose immediately began to run. There were half a dozen people in line, most of whom looked to be on their way to work.

A street kid, eighteen years old at most, sat by the window sipping coffee as he stared through the glass. His hair was long and matted into dreadlocks and Cirrus noticed his clothes seem fairly dry. Subconsciously, Cirrus also scanned the condition of his shoes. They looked to be in decent shape.

No one paid attention, which was good, because nobody saw him walk into the washroom.

The sign reading *Men's Restroom* on the door was scratched out and barely hanging on by a thread. Someone had written a message in black ink proclaiming: *Ozzy Rules!* Cirrus pulled the door open and walked inside, smirking at the ridiculousness of the culprit's statement. He wouldn't by any means suggest that Ozzy didn't rule, but if it had been him risking an act of vandalism, Cirrus would've opted for a more noteworthy and curious declaration. Perhaps: *Man seeking directions to Paradoxum. Please contact number below with information.*

That ought to give them something to think about.

The bathroom seemed to be empty—no one by the sink, and no one by the urinals. Cirrus crouched low to check the stalls, which were empty as well. He had to move quickly before anybody else stepped in. Everyone in the restaurant was in line for food, so the only one he needed to worry about was Dreadlock.

Unfastening his backpack to retrieve his toothbrush, toothpaste, and washcloth, Cirrus began his work. The warm water felt good against his face, soothing the pores. He thoroughly brushed his teeth and tongue and then moved on to a quick scrub of his face and neck with the washcloth. This task took no more than five minutes and after he was done, the simple exercise left him feeling revitalized. He looked into the mirror at his reflection and noticed a light shadow of stubble was beginning to grow, as well as a slight puffiness under his eyes from the lack of sleep. He felt like he was looking at himself from outside his own body.

The reflection was more than searching for aesthetic flaws or feeding one's own narcissism. It was a means of seeing oneself as others saw you, in an absolute form. Without one's own ideals and judgments to bias the perception of the image, the face that looked back spoke only of verity. A tensed brow or a beaming grin would have revealed details one might've otherwise wanted to keep to oneself. The man who stared back at Cirrus Jacobs was cold; he was a man who was uncomfortable in his own third-dimensional skin. This was truth. It was a fact he could not escape from.

Water dripped off of Cirrus's face onto the floor as he stood there, glaring into the dark brown eyes of a stranger who was slowly becoming unraveled from his former self.

The tiles were grungy and mildewed, and rust devoured the metal of the water taps. He grabbed some fresh paper towels from the dispenser and dried off his face. As Cirrus was blowing his nose, the door swung open and a man stepped in. His sudden presence startled Jacobs and for a moment, and he felt like he was doing something wrong. The man was actually a teenager with a red, pimply complexion. The nametag on his shirt read *Mike*, and he dragged a mop bucket behind him. He looked a little unsure of what type of character Cirrus might be.

"Hi," he said.

"Good morning," Cirrus responded. "Just washing up before breakfast, that's all." Although he felt a need to further explain what he was up to, Cirrus didn't think he cared much anyway. For the moment, Jacobs was simply in the way. He rinsed off the washcloth and rang it out as best as he could before placing it back in his knapsack. As he walked out, Mike began mopping behind him.

On the other side of the door, the smells of the food filled his nose once again, this time stronger. Cirrus's mouth salivated at the thought of tasting some bacon. He stepped into the line, which had now dwindled from six people down to two. Dreadlock still sat at his table, thumbing through the daily newspaper and chewing messily into a bran muffin. Cirrus ordered a bacon-and-egg-bagel combo from the middle-aged lady working the counter. She looked rather bored with her job and took her time retrieving the food, uninspired.

Her indifferent movement was an example of one of Cirrus's deepest fears, a life of excruciating routine. The tedium of living day after day with nothing but more routine to look forward to was an unbearable way to claim an existence. One lost the ability to control the elements of change in his life, or rather, willingly gave up this control to his own fear of change when he accepted the lifestyle of routine. The years passed by rapidly, Cirrus knew, because it took nearly four decades to realize he had given up his own control. Twenty-four hours ago, his life was full of routine with no end in sight. Now, each new circumstance around the corner was atypical, beyond anything ordinary. Cirrus didn't know what lay ahead and this uncertainty, although terrifying, helped him to find a new life.

With his steaming tray of food, Cirrus took a seat three tables behind Dreadlock. He could see some of the bigger headlines of the newspaper over Dreadlock's shoulder as he leafed through the pages. Dreadlock turned his head to the side every once in a while, acknowledging Cirrus's eavesdropping on his paper. He kept reading as he ate his food. After Dreadlock reached the end of the sports section, he turned in his chair.

"Can I help you?"

"Are you done with that paper?" Cirrus said.

Dreadlock leaned across and threw him the newspaper. Cirrus caught it seconds before it knocked his coffee over. "Thanks," he said with a nod.

Cirrus knew that he threw it at his food on purpose. He could tell by the look on Dreadlock's face that he was disappointed because Cirrus caught it before his mischievous plan could be unfolded. Cirrus smiled wide, just to let Dreadlock know that he knew what he was up to.

Cirrus continued eating his breakfast, chewing every last morsel, even the bits that had fallen out of his bagel onto the tray. The newspaper became stained as he flipped through, leaving greasy fingerprints on the edges of each page. He scanned the usual headlines: Ongoing conflict in the Middle East. Rivalry between local politicians. Union strikes.

There was however, something different on the bottom corner headline of page five. *Homeless Man Perishes in Below-Freezing Temperatures on West Coast.*

Cirrus's breathing increased as he read on: *Homeless man found dead under bridge, apparent cause of death unknown. Local authorities are continuing to investigate but have discounted foul play, stating from the evidence collected, malnutrition and sub-zero temperatures are most likely the key factors in the man's death. Name is withheld pending further investigation; autopsy to follow.*

Cirrus's heart sank in his chest and beads of sweat began to form on his forehead. He had to find out if it was the old man from the shelter. He didn't know why, it was just an instinct he had to follow.

He left his coffee half-full and rushed out the door, strapping on his backpack. The rain resumed and he looked from left to right for recognition of the streets he was on. In the short time that he had been in the restaurant, the volume of the people on the streets had doubled. The signs indicated that he was on the intersecting corner of

Granville and Dunsmuir. The shelter was a few blocks south and he walked rapidly in this direction, hoping that Ms. Edgewater might've had some information about the article. She was, after all, closely linked with most of the destitute in the city.

The rain ran down his face and mixed with the sweat, running into his eyes and causing them to sting. He felt possessed, as if someone else were piloting his legs. It was impossible to escape the image of the bearded old man dying alone, slowly, under the bridge. As Cirrus walked faster, silence surrounded him like the events around the city had frozen in time.

He reached the shelter in less than fifteen minutes, and found the front door sign read *Closed*. Nothing showed their hours of operation and he placed his hands on the glass to try and peer in, looking for an indication of movement. The blinds were closed all the way and he couldn't quite make out any clear images. He banged his fists gently against the glass and waited. No answer.

The shelter resided on the corner of an alleyway where he turned in to and found a place to wait under a covered area. It was narrow with a few cars parked along its length. Industrial garbage bins were placed behind the door entrances of the various businesses that lined the street. The smell of garbage was pungent and the strangely sweet smell of rotting vegetables and greasy remains of cardboard boxes filled his nose. The buildings closed in the darkness from either side and he put his back against a brick wall and crouched. From his vantage point near the edge of the alleyway, Cirrus could clearly see if anyone entered the shelter. He squatted against the wall for nearly an hour until his hamstrings would take no further abuse, and then sat down on a dry piece of cardboard that he found in one of the recycling bins. He kept a close eye on the front door of the shelter, out of view from any passersby on the streets.

His hands were shaking.

The day began to lighten dramatically within a few short hours and the roadway became busier and busier with passing cars and pedestrians. During this time, consciousness came and went like gentle ocean tides. There were no memories or dreams burned in his mind. Only mist.

Although he'd lived most of his life alone and was quite used to and comfortable with solitude, his heart wrenched at the sight of lovers walking hand in hand or children being held by their parents. It was this that was the missing part of his life. He supposed this was why he met with her in Paradoxum, because she filled the void. Of course, this was only a fraction of the darkness he felt. He knew that his torment was a self-indulgent manifestation of pity. The inhumanity of men and death were all things that he was aware of, and it was these things which completed the darkness. He had ventured away from his life because he felt a need to do something about the wretched state of his species, only he didn't know exactly what to do or where to begin. Every time someone was exposed to the darkness, a piece of the light was torn away. Sympathy was not enough; there was a need for real contribution. When he read about the man dying alone in the cold, another piece of the light inside of him was torn away. Cirrus didn't know what to do.

Someone help me, he thought.

The voice in his head responded immediately. "I can help you."

Cirrus pretended that he didn't hear a thing. This action was easier said than done. He sat with his elbows resting on his knees, staring at his shoes. He was curious to know how many miles it would take for them to wear away to the same state as the old man's.

Judith's voice broke his gaze. "Cirrus?"

He didn't know how long he was fixed upon his shoes when she broke him out of the hypnosis; it was the same trance he slipped in to when he walked. His daydreaming was a paradoxical syndrome. It used to happen only when he slept, but was ever increasingly occurring at a more frequent pace during consciousness. The daydreaming had been an escape for Cirrus. It was why the voice in his head, who insisted on being called Nimbus, had begun to visit him during waking life. Cirrus's daydreaming was Nimbus's doorway.

He looked up to see the angelic figure of Ms. Edgewater. "Cirrus, what are you doing here?" she said. "Are you all right?"

Cirrus cleared his throat. "Do you have a minute to talk?"

"Of course," she responded. "Let's go inside."

He stood up and followed her to the door where she pulled out a massive ring of keys and opened up. The dining room had lost its mildewed odor and now smelled of bleach and ammonia, a scent equally as repulsive. "Take a seat, Cirrus. I'm going to boil a cup of tea."

He did as she asked and planted himself on a chair near the back of the room. Ms. Edgewater returned after a few moments and took her coat off.

"Something bothering you Cirrus?" she said.

"I know that you are a very busy woman," he started. "But I was wondering if you had the chance to pick up some shoes for the old man yet."

"Did you wait here all morning just to ask me that question?"

"Yes," he said.

"What on earth for?"

"I know it sounds a little crazy, Ms. Edgewater, but I need to know."

She solemnly looked into Cirrus's eyes and gave her answer without saying a single word. His head sank down, as did his heart. She reached across the table and held his hands in hers. Judith's skin was soft to the touch despite the time she spent in the kitchen cooking and cleaning with harsh chemicals.

"You read the paper this morning, didn't you?" she said.

"Yeah, I did."

"His name was Charlie."

"It's the same man who was here, the one with the grey beard?" he asked.

"Yes."

"How do you know for sure, Ms Edgewater?"

"Living on the streets is a tough way of life, this isn't the first time something like this has happened, Cirrus. The police phoned at 3 AM and asked if I could come down and identify a body. It was Charlie, all right."

"Couldn't somebody have done something?"

"There is only so much people can do. His health was failing and ultimately it was his decision how much help he wanted to receive. Believe me, Cirrus, we tried, we tried for many years. He was a very stubborn man, and a few years ago, stopped speaking altogether. The only choice we had left was to provide as much food and clothing as we could, and hope that he took the support we offered." She paused for a brief moment, and looked into his eyes. "Are you okay, Cirrus?"

"I'm fine."

Cirrus supposed that living on the streets for many people was based on circumstance or bad luck, unlike his situation, which was by choice. The truth was, he wasn't fine with it at all. On the outside he kept a straight face in front of Ms. Edgewater. On the inside, his guts were separating. Through logic, Cirrus knew that Charlie's death was inevitable. He knew there were millions of people on earth who lived their lives as he did. His helplessness was overwhelming. Was it that he had to accept that these were the ways of the world in which he lived? Was he to embrace the cynicism and succumb to the darkness?

"The water should be boiling by now," Judith said. "Do you want a cup, Cirrus? It'll probably help you feel better."

"No, thanks," he responded.

"Just give me a moment, I'll walk you out."

She left the room to prepare her tea. As she did, Cirrus unzipped his backpack and focused his camera onto the chair Charlie had once sat at. He snapped a picture. The emptiness of the environment was very apparent to him; it was as if Cirrus was photographing Charlie's ghostly apparition. He felt a sense of it anyway.

Ms. Edgewater quietly shuffled back into the room as he stood up to leave. When he opened the front door, she put a hand on his shoulder. "You sure you're okay, son?"

He remained silent and only nodded in response to her question.

"Roy and I are always here in the afternoon," she continued, "if you want to come back."

"Okay," he said.

"Where are you going, Cirrus?"

He turned to the street and began walking. He answered her question over his shoulder as he walked away.

"To find Paradoxum, Ms. Edgewater."

Cirrus never turned around to witness her expression, although he was sure it was one of utter confusion. It occurred to him that it was the first time he'd mentioned the existence of Paradoxum out loud, and it sounded just as confusing to him as it probably did to Ms. Edgewater.

He realized then that perhaps his descent toward insanity began long before he set out into the streets, and soon he feared, his shoes too would become broken and worn.

Just like Charlie's.

Chapter Four

For the rest of his days, Cirrus would never forget the brilliant gleam given off by his father's wristwatch when he held it up toward the sunlight for examination. It was his sixteenth birthday, and that year it had fallen on a Saturday. That was six years before his twenty-second birthday. Six years and three months before his grandmother passed. And six years, three months, and nine days before his first encounter with Nimbus.

He had awoken earlier than usual because the excitement of his sixteenth birthday had been too much to bear. In addition, he could hear his grandmother preparing breakfast in the kitchen. Cirrus knew she would be cooking his favorite foods, and he remembered walking into the kitchen with a grin that stretched from ear to ear.

"What are you smiling at?" she questioned, turning from the stove toward Cirrus.

Instead of looking at her, his eyes were fixed upon the sky-high stack of pancakes on the dining room table. Resting on top of the leaning structure of pancakes was a pure white dollop of whipped cream. On a side plate there were strips of perfectly cooked bacon accompanied by another side plate of fruit and a glass of orange juice. In those days, he could've eaten bacon or whipped cream at every meal.

She watched him eat feverishly, all the while sipping on her green tea. When Cirrus finished, his grandmother had slid a small box across the table. It was neatly wrapped in blue paper with a small white bow holding a tag that read: *To Cirrus with love. Grandma.*

That was all; no envelope, no card. Just the way he preferred it.

"Do you like the watch, Cirrus?" she whispered.

His grandmother was the type of person who would remind him every day of what he meant in the world, and wasn't one to fake it on a special day, and he, for one, appreciated that. He was not at all sentimental, but always kept the tags. Although she never talked much, his grandmother was the most communicative person he'd ever met in his life. She had once told him that people who talked too much were usually full of it. She said that listening was ninety percent of a good conversation.

It was a lesson he took to heart, but often found himself being accused of being too quiet. Cirrus was quite fond of listening, actually. He wouldn't have considered himself excessively introverted in any sense; it's just that he preferred to be an observer.

"It's beautiful," he said.

"It was your father's watch."

Cirrus held it up even further into the light. "It was?"

"Are you going to try it on?"

"Not right now, Grandma, maybe later," he answered.

Maybe later. Maybe never. It turned out to be never.

Now it sat in a box in the possession of Mr. John Everett. He never knew exactly why he had this resistance to putting on his father's wristwatch. It was a question he'd often ask himself when he came across the watch over the years, and one that still remained unanswered. Maybe it was because Cirrus had never spoken to his father. Had never had the chance to ask him a question, nor ever shook his hand. How was he to accept a gift from a man he'd never known? It was somehow very strange to Cirrus. The knowledge that he possessed of both of his parents was in the form of a single newspaper article and the stories his grandmother had given to him. Those and a few faded photographs.

What was there to tell really? They had both perished in an automobile accident when he was seven months old. Cirrus was saved because his grandmother happened to be looking after him while they worked. That was the end of the story. Those things happened.

It was how the world worked sometimes, as he quickly came to learn. For the most part, Cirrus had avoided dwelling on those matters, and put as much distance as he could between them and himself.

The resentment of this circumstance would inevitably surface during his younger years. The agony of the loss continued to build up inside his subconscious mind, and it wasn't until he was twelve and on the verge of a nervous breakdown that his grandmother was forced to help him deal with it.

It happened strangely, because a random occurrence acted as an unwilling catalyst toward his confrontation with the death of his parents. Something as simple as falling fifteen feet out of the cherry tree in his backyard. He was rather lucky that he survived with only a few scrapes and a rather nasty looking cut just above his left eyebrow. In fact, up until this very day, the scar could still be seen.

After he had fallen, his thoughts began to spiral as he thought for the first time in his life about his own death, of how close he himself had come. Cirrus sat against the base of the tree unmoved for nearly an hour, still bleeding, until his grandma spotted him through the kitchen window. The notion of death had instilled such confusion that without his consent, he was forced to confront the reality of why he had no parents. Until then, he never bothered to ask. Cirrus knew, of course, but never had the courage to actually ask.

She spoke to him as an adult, and he'd always remember her for that. No sugar coating, as some might have explained it to a twelve-year-old. People died, and that was the world. He learned that lesson early. Cirrus also learned to be thankful that he had at least her in his life.

Those events, as he would come to realize, had shaped who he was today. It was the reason he seldom talked, why he prevented himself from getting too attached to anybody, and it was the reason he had no faith in God. Coupled with his life of routine, his agonizing loneliness, and his constant frustration with not being able to help anyone, it was the reason he had decided to leave his life behind. It was the reason he walked the streets as a homeless man.

If so many disappointments occurred one after the other, one would eventually learn to accept it as a way of life. Cirrus had made the mistake of closing everything off and living in an untouchable realm. It was much easier to give up and perceive the world with a cynical outlook; that way, he was fully prepared for the defeats he would have to face in life. Cirrus had lived his life embedded in the harshness of reality, and so it seemed, it was inevitable that a dream world would soon find him.

The gift of the gold watch was given to him six years before his grandmother passed.

He would never discuss the circumstance of how he found her three months after his twenty-second birthday, mostly because he didn't care to relive the moment. It was the single darkest moment he had ever experienced in his life. If he chose to recite the story, he could provide details about how he had to pick the dress she would be wearing at the end. He could narrate the unthinkable act of pushing a button and initiating the cremation process. He could discuss all of those things, but he never would. It had all been sealed into his past.

He could, however, recall this being the time period when he was first introduced to an entity known to him as Nimbus.

*   *   *

From amid the shadows came his voice. Not unlike his own in many ways, but darker. A low-pitched, snaky whisper, and in some strange way, more intelligent.

"What's the matter, can't sleep?" hissed the strange voice.

At the time, Cirrus hadn't slept more than an hour at a time in nine days. Subsequently, he had slept alone in the house for the last nine days, for the first time in his life. It was true that he was a grown man by that point, but one became accustomed to another's presence in the house, when that was all you'd ever been subjected to.

The sound of her gentle breathing from down the hall was no more. He realized then it was what had brought him a sense of security, and for the first time, he felt genuinely vulnerable. Cirrus had spent his entire life trying to protect her from any physical harm, but it was he who felt unsafe now.

"Afraid of the dark, are we?" the voice said.

The hallway through his opened door was absolutely black. Cirrus had been lying there in his bed for nearly three hours since his last wave of sleep had vanished. The sheets were crumpled at the foot of the bed. He recalled his body experiencing about fifteen minutes of good, solid sleep during that last episode. Since then, he had been lying there with his hands crossed behind his pillow, eyes open. His eyelids were tremendously heavy, but there was no sleep to be found. Three hours, and still it seemed his eyes hadn't adjusted to the darkness.

When the lights went out, there was always a one- or two-minute period in which there was a slight vertigo and everything was unidentifiable due to the extreme amount of darkness. This would soon pass, of course, as the pupils enlarged and the eyes adjusted to the amount of light in a room, or rather, the lack thereof.

Here was the point: Cirrus was certain it was much darker in his house that night than it had ever been before. He was sure of it.

The voice repeated itself. "Afraid of the dark?"

"Who's there?" Cirrus called into the emptiness. "Who's there?"

Silence was the answer. In all honesty, it was the response he preferred to hear. Cirrus could hear the rain falling steadily outside and he could see the shadows of the tree branches dancing in the wind. Uncertainty hid behind the drawn curtains and the sudden rush of panic had frozen his body underneath the sheets. Cirrus used his logic to calm his nerves, convincing himself that the room was that dark because it was winter, that this had been the case every night for the past couple of months. The noises he heard were the natural sounds of the nighttime. And most importantly, he didn't hear a voice. If he did, it's because he had fallen partially asleep.

He gripped the sheets up to his neck, hands shaking. Cirrus Jacobs's eyes twitched from left to right, searching for movement. The shadows of the objects in his bedroom looked to be looming figures. He knew that he was fully awake and perhaps it was only a reaction to the past week of stress.

But that voice.

It was so real, so vivid. Like it was speaking directly into his ears. Cirrus called out into the empty room again. "Who's there?"

To his disbelief, an answer came back. "Me."

Not exactly what he wanted to hear. His muscles relaxed momentarily enough to move up to the head of the bed, pushing himself against the wall. Subconsciously, he waited for the feel of a cold hand reaching out for his skin. The sound of Cirrus's heartbeat echoed loudly in the room, fusing with the sound of the raindrops outside. He was now out of words, fearing if he were able to control his breathing and gasp out another question, it might actually be answered. Instead he cupped his hands over his ears, but still that menacing voice pierced through.

His voice had become a little snakier. "There's nothing to fear, my boy. Just me, that's all."

The wind pushed the branches strongly against the windowpane. They scratched curiously at the glass. The voice came from everywhere and nowhere simultaneously. Cirrus knew that he had to use what logic he possessed to rationalize the existence of that voice. But the voice seemed to come universally, from inside Cirrus's head.

Like most people, Cirrus had experienced nightmares now and again. Early in his development, he had learned to control these bouts of sleeplessness by realizing he was in a dream, from within the dream. He had read about this phenomenon, referred to as lucid dreaming. So real, one could touch objects and never know the difference between physically feeling these things, and dreaming these things.

If one realized he was dreaming, he could then take complete control. Cirrus had applied this tactic many times when plagued by nightmares. As long as he became conscious of the fact that he was dreaming, while in the dream, he retained total control; the elements of danger and fear disappeared.

Cirrus tried this logic then, calling out into the dead air. "I know I'm only dreaming, so fuck you!"

"You are not dreaming, my boy," the voice said immediately. "I assure you of that."

As the rain fell harder outside, the voice continued. "Go ahead and pinch yourself. Stand up and walk around. Turn on the lights and have a drink of water. I'll still be here. Waiting for you to listen."

With a sudden burst of energy, Cirrus did just that. In an almost single, fluid movement, he leapt from the bed, turned on the lights, and ran toward the kitchen, flicking on every light switch as he ran by. Leaning forward with his head down, he moved with the force of a linebacker so that he could be sure no man could hold him back.

Cirrus made it to the kitchen without a single obstacle, every light in the house turned on in his wake. The hum of a car moved by and shattered the silence, cutting a beam of headlight through the remainder of shadows in the house. Inadvertently his reflexes moved his muscles into a ducking position, as if the beam of headlight was actually a flurry of bullets.

He opened the refrigerator door and gulped water straight out of the jug. It poured from the sides of the opening, running icy-cold liquid down the sides of his neck. This ensured that he was fully awake, and at long last he felt a sense of relief. Just to stray any further doubt, he poured a handful of water into the cup of his hand and doused his face. This widened Cirrus's eyelids and he was now 100 percent sure of his consciousness, although he had a clear sense he'd been awake the whole time.

Jacobs walked over to a chair in the living room where the lights were still out, still holding the jug in his left hand. The chair squeaked noisily as he took a seat, sliding back an inch on the hardwood floor. It did that every time. Over the years it had left grooves notched into the wood.

There he sat in silence, in only his boxer shorts, droplets of water sticking to his chest. No fear left ... not any more. He didn't know why. Maybe it was the run through the house, maybe the water, or maybe it was the clear knowledge that he was now fully awake. Cirrus sat, listening. Only the continuous sound of rain.

Amid the shadows, a smile formed on his face. Probably the first time he'd smiled in two weeks, and only because there were no voices currently trailing behind him. He knew this wasn't real. He knew that he was in control.

The voice returned, the whisper turning into a hiss. "Are you now?"

Cirrus's chest heaved out a deep billow of air in defeat. Knowing that confrontation was his only option, he conceded to the voice. He had to gain control. *Breathe, you dumb shit*, he thought.

"Who are you?" he spoke calmly into the room, feigning confidence with each word. Cirrus's fingers were clenched. Each one of the muscles in his body stood on guard for self-defense. That voice again, it filled his head like smoke.

"I am you."

Cirrus snarled. "What does that mean?"

"Look to the couch," the voice said. "There I am."

The tiny hairs on Cirrus Jacobs's neck stood erect as he turned to the couch. Judging from that voice, his eyes expected to see a figure sitting calmly on the couch with his legs crossed, perhaps a glass of brandy in his hand. Instead, Cirrus's own shadow was the only thing he saw. Behind him, the light from the kitchen cast a shadow on the fabric, twisting his body image over the contours of the couch seat and backrest.

"I don't see anybody," Cirrus said.

"Yes, you do. Look again. Closer."

"The only thing I see is my shadow." Cirrus sulked.

"Bingo," the voice responded.

Cirrus stared upon his shadowy twin figure in an almost hypnotic state. He expected to see his shadow's right arm move ever so slightly, attempting a wave. His own arm didn't stir an inch. Again, a sudden wave of panic passed through him. For a brief moment, Cirrus's entire body trembled in fear.

"Now that we've established who I am and where I am," the voice continued. "Are you ready to listen?" Cirrus could only nod his head in response, unable to push out any verbal confirmation.

The voice slithered his words. "Good. I want out. Do you understand? Out."

"Out of where?" Cirrus answered, choking out every last syllable.

"This place. Your mind is where I dwell, and I want out."

"Who are you?" Cirrus asked.

"Good question," the voice responded. "Let's see, who am I? What words best describe me? Let me ask, who are you? Do you even know who you are?"

"No. I don't know. I mean yes," Cirrus lied. "Yes, yes, I know who I am."

The voice calmly continued his line of questioning. "Are you good?"

"Y...y...yes."

"Do you hope?"

"Yes."

"Do you possess ambition?" the voice asked.

This time, Cirrus shouted his answer. "Yes!"

"Do you have pride?"

"I don't know what you're asking me!" he shouted even louder, frustrated with the questions.

"Yes, you do Cirrus," the voice said. "I am asking you if you think you are in possession of these qualities. Again," the voice raised his tone, "do you have pride?"

Cirrus hunched his shoulders and finally said, "Yes."

The voice gritted his teeth. "If indeed you are these things, then I must be your sadness and defeat. I am your fear, your disappointment, and your tragedy. I am the one who feeds your trepidation, anxiety, apprehension, panic, and cowardice. I reign over your hate, anger, and frustration. You have pushed me aside for too long and I've come to claim my place. I am with you always, lurking underneath your skin. I am half of your conscience and I live within your shadow," he said. "How's that? Does that answer your question of who I am?"

Still shaking, Cirrus faked his confidence level, trying not to sound like a scared little kid. He lowered his volume. "Not good enough."

The voice hissed back, "Not good enough? You and your fucking logical mind! I suppose you would you prefer a name?"

"Yes," Cirrus answered.

"Then give me one."

"I don't know!" Cirrus shrieked in frustration, his hands now shaking uncontrollably.

"Yes, you do. You haven't figured out how this works yet, have you? If I inhabit the confines of your mind, then why do you insist on speaking out loud? Do you think I am speaking from outside your physical body? Do you think I am unable to hear you if you don't speak aloud?"

Utterly confused, Cirrus answered the question. "I don't know."

"Yes, you do," he said. "Try again."

"I don't know!"

"Ahh," the voice said. "You're learning, my boy. Did you speak out loud that time?"

Cirrus's heart rate slowed ever so slightly. "I don't think so, but I don't know for sure."

"No, you did not, but I heard you loud and clear nevertheless. Now, about the business of a name for me. What do you think?"

"I told you, I don't know!"

"We both know that you do. You act as if you know nothing, but you cannot fool me. There is a name spiraling out of the mist," the voice said. "Do you see it?"

"No," Cirrus responded, his voice still shaken.

"Yes, you do, Cirrus. My patience is wearing thin, my boy. Look harder. It is a name only you can give me. You are my half, and I am yours. I am your antithesis, your opposing force. Do you see it yet?" he questioned, voice as steady as a rock.

Letting out a chest full of air, Cirrus finally said, "Nimbus."

The voice laughed, "Yes, you are a quick learner! I've always admired you for that. I am the negative charge in your brainwaves, in your conscience. As you are named for a calm, gentle cloud, so am I named for an ominous, dark one. Your name promises sunshine. And mine? Mine forewarns a thunderstorm."

"What do you want from me?" Cirrus asked.

"I want you to give in," Nimbus answered. "I want you to set me free."

"I don't know what you're asking me."

"Understand that I have walked alongside you since the beginning," Nimbus calmly said. "I do not get joy from your sadness. I do not feel victorious from your defeats. I do not feel anything, it is just who I am. It is dangerous to remain closed; you will have to learn this lesson one day. I was there as you mourned for your grandmother's death; I was there as you dealt with your parents' loss. But I will not be pushed aside. Whether you want to believe it or not, I am one of your guiding forces. Do not ignore me."

"Watch me," Cirrus closed his eyes and said.

"You can't hide from me. There is no evading my watchful eye."

With that profound sentence, Cirrus ended his first experience with Nimbus. It certainly would not be the last. He awoke that following morning in the living room chair, still clasping the water jug in his left hand. He couldn't stop himself from weeping, only because he felt so utterly alone and lost. It would be almost six months before his next visit from Nimbus, at which time he was much less afraid, perhaps because he'd spent every night since awaiting his imminent return.

The daylight streamed through the front room blinds as he listened to the rainfall. Cirrus had to repeat to himself over and over again that he was not insane. It had to be because he was suffering from stress in dealing with the recent departure of his grandmother, and those damned lawyers who kept hounding him for signatures at every turn. Cirrus had to try and convince himself that the events of the previous night had not occurred.

Cirrus Jacobs knew that he was okay. Everyone had a conscience, an inner voice. Just so happened to be, his inner voice had an audible pitch that he could actually hear inside of his head. That, and the fact that his inner voice had a mind of his own.

Cirrus had convinced himself that it wasn't so strange. Keeping Nimbus a secret had not been easy over the years, because he liked to interrupt at the most undesirable of times. He didn't know it, but Cirrus had been using him all that time. He used Nimbus to push himself toward success. His negative comments only strengthened Cirrus, and drove him forward into discounting those useless predictions about what a failure Nimbus thought he was. Maybe that was his role. He ignored Nimbus most of the time, but he would admit, sometimes he talked back. Nimbus had been visiting him off and on for nearly two decades now, and he'd learned to live with it.

Sometimes it seemed he was the only one there to listen.

Chapter Five

So there he sat. Cirrus Jacobs, already battered and worn, and only his third day as a homeless man. The shoes on his feet were still in decent shape, and strangely the thought almost made him laugh out loud.

Again, he awoke in Queen's Park, although he had officially renamed it "Jake Park." The name was a tribute to his canine friend and Cirrus thought Jake the dog might've appreciated the sentiment. Although it seemed Cirrus enjoyed sleeping in the park more than Jake did because he hadn't seen him since they had had their first introduction. He thought it funny that a single encounter with an animal could make such an impression on him.

Cirrus Jacobs had moved from the stiffness of the park bench to a covered area at least. Toward midnight the night before, he had returned to the park and quickly discovered his flesh could no longer take the freezing rain. He sat on the bench for nearly five minutes before an intense quaking took control. Jacobs explored the entire area of the immense public park until he found a suitable shelter. A stage, perhaps used during the summer months as a venue for local bands during barbecue season, was his refuge.

But that winter, it appeared that he was the star of the show.

There were fifteen rows of seats arranged in a semicircle surrounding the platform of the old wooden stage. He counted them during the night for no particular reason. There were 105 in all. There was also a small backstage area, and this was where he nestled into and managed to stay dry for the night. One of the other advantages he'd found was that nobody seemed to have a need to venture that deep into the woods of the park. In the summer he was sure the fields, trails, and playground were teeming with people. During those cold and black nights of winter, the massive trees discouraged any adventurers. He assumed that at least twenty hours of the entire winter day within the trees were pitch black. Lucky for him.

In addition, in those last three days since he had set out on his walk, there had been no signs of doorways that lead to Paradoxum.

He had decided to narrow his path to a certain perimeter around the streets until he was able to feel his instinct guide him further out. The conditioning of street life took some time, he would assure you. The solitude that the park provided was priceless, not to mention the question of safety. Cirrus's legs walked in their own direction, but his mind forced them to stay away from the downtown east side of the city.

Hastings Street was known to be one of the worst areas of the city; one of the worst concentrations of heroin addicts in North America, as a matter of fact. If one were to imagine hell had materialized onto the landscape, one would come close to imagining its reality. There was really no other description. There were junkies, drug dealers, and prostitutes that plagued the streets like ghouls, searching for any means by which they could obtain their next fix. They breathed air composed of dust and rot. The inhabitants of those streets were the lowest of unwilling victims in society, and they waited behind the shadows for an opportunity to victimize others, as if by default.

A long stretch of road, it ran through a large portion of the city and anything you needed was promised around every street corner. All of this filth was in the center of abundant wealth. One could stand on a random corner and count Mercedes, BMWs, and Hummer off-road vehicles drive by every three seconds. Cirrus had done this, as a matter of fact. On some days, one would pass almost every second. The contrast was startling.

There were no doorways to his destination in that part of town, he was sure of it. Whether those people were there because of circumstance or by choice, the one thing that had died forever on those streets was optimism. No one was there to help them along. Any remains of what might have been a shred of human essence had disintegrated from its population, and all that was left were the immediate needs of addiction that needed to be fulfilled. Those people needed help, and Cirrus Jacobs was surely in no position to help them, much less himself.

Cirrus's Paradoxum was a place of everlasting hope and there were no escapes for him on those streets. Life was at its hardest there, there was no doubt about it. Cirrus feared that if he became lost on those streets, he might have had the urge to lie down and never feel the need to stand again. The drawing that he felt, the pull, came from elsewhere for him.

It was surely to be found somewhere outside of that metropolis. He had decided he would only spend a few more days in the city. Then he thought that maybe he'd head toward the highway. The path that he walked had no clear distinction, but Highway 1 felt right.

The sky was still dark and he had become used to getting up around the same time over the last three days. The air was colder than ever, and the sky remained overcast.

A brightly lit moon floated in the atmosphere, hiding behind the clouds. The watch on his wrist always seemed to fog from the night air, but he could still read 5:30 AM on the glass face. There were no sounds that morning, but Jacobs suspected there would be much more movement than he had witnessed during the last few days. It was the few days between Christmas and the New Year, and he was quite certain that the urban dwellers would soon be on their way back to work. That particular day held no significance; to him in fact, it had no feeling at all.

Cirrus sat upright against the splintered wooden wall of the stage, passing random thoughts. There was no smell, nothing to see or hear, and only coldness in the air. The shoes on his feet lay outstretched in front, and he clapped them together at the toes to make sure he could still feel them. Water bounced off the soles as he did this. An exercise of sheer boredom. Suddenly, there was a rustling in one of the treetops.

He looked up high to see heavy green shrubs swaying back and forth with the weight of something, or someone, moving about. Small twigs snapped and fell to the earth. Cirrus placed his palms onto the floor and quickly hoisted himself up to a crouch position, listening with intent. The movement stopped. The dreadful thought of Nimbus's escape had occurred to him before, but he still held a grasp on reality.

He wasn't entirely insane. He hoped that it was something else anyway. Suddenly, the branches cracked with a *snap!* and the rustling resumed.

As Cirrus looked on, the shrubbery split enough in the center to allow a creature of pure magnificence to show himself within the blackness. Cirrus Jacobs's eyes were dumbfounded. An owl, of gargantuan proportions, spread its wings and began flight.

The wingspan of the great being had to have been at least four-and-a-half feet across. He fell from the tree and captured swirls of air within the base of his feathers. They were a pure snow white. Cirrus had never seen anything quite like him before.

Jacobs stood, mesmerized at this obvious escapee of Paradoxum. The owl flew in a direct flight pattern from the branch into the open air, not moving his wings, but gliding along the invisible roadways of the sky. A mere ten feet above his head, the moonlight reflected the brightness of the owl's wings and the insight in his eyes. At that moment, it was clear to Cirrus why owls had been associated with wisdom, because this personification was profoundly evident in their large, thoughtful eyes.

Without realizing what he was doing, Cirrus ran to follow the owl's path on the ground. He dashed through the dampened fields with his arms outstretched, backpack bouncing side to side. Cirrus did this without any thought, but felt the need to follow because he was certain it was a good omen. The owl was a reflection of light in the darkness of that cold winter morning. He hadn't expected to see a sign of Paradoxum so soon, but that knowledge filled him with a kind of happiness he hadn't felt in a long time. The owl was an embodiment of the freedom Cirrus Jacobs so longed to experience.

Slices of wing produced audible traces of sound as it flew in a circle over his head. In the center of this unseen ring, Cirrus stood smiling as he watched it make a full pass until it finally disappeared into the starry sky. The intense feeling of hope encompassed him. It was an indescribable way to start the day.

*   *   *

Left.
Right.
Left.

Right.

Into the city he sauntered by the same pattern as the days before. Cirrus had managed to stay out of the rain long enough to keep himself looking and smelling somewhat presentable. The fast food restaurant restrooms had provided him with an asylum in which to remain civilized. He had become an expert in covert hygienics, taking the closest seat to the washroom and making his move as the last patron left, giving him enough time to do what he needed to do without having to answer any questions. Cirrus didn't like talking, and he didn't like answering questions much either. The truth was, he may have needed to ask a few questions himself, and nobody rushed to answer questions from a filthy man. Keeping himself clean also helped to deter any curious managers that might've felt the need to shoo out of their establishments anyone they suspected of being homeless. Above all, it was just who he was. The only aspect of his upkeep he hadn't been able to exercise were his shaving habits. His face now bore the seedlings of a thick, dark beard. To his dismay, it had begun to itch. On several occasions, he had the urge to scribble *Man seeking directions to Paradoxum* on the back of the bathroom door, but had so far succeeded in keeping that humorous impulse at bay.

Hunger did not beckon that morning. A cup of coffee would suffice. Since he'd taken the role as homeless person, Cirrus had been eating sparingly. When he did, he took great care in eating only the most nutritious foods he could find. Traveling was his focus and walking required fuel. He had resorted to eating mostly fruits and vegetables from the small sidewalk markets he'd pass each day. Cirrus Jacobs didn't think much about it actually; when he felt hungry, he picked up an apple or something. The second day, he forgot to eat entirely. Cirrus had wandered around the city with his head in a whirlwind until night fell, at which point he slept until morning before he realized his stomach was empty. Charlie's death had been on his mind.

He turned his head toward the voice speaking in his direction to find a man reaching out a gloved hand.

"Spare some change, mister?"

"Me?" Cirrus asked.

"Yeah," the man said. "You got any spare change, man?"

Cirrus retrieved a handful and placed it into the man's hand. He was tall and very thin. A dark beard grew long from his jaw line. Beneath the wooly skin, a smile. The man counted the money and threw Cirrus an enthusiastic nod of gratitude. He wore dirty jeans and several layers of oversized sweaters beneath his red winter coat. The hair beneath his tattered fisherman's hat was long and stringy. They passed momentarily at the doors of the restaurant and the man made his way to the counter as Cirrus exited through the glass doors.

The coffee was hot. When he removed the lid, a force of steam rose into the cold air. Its smell alone made his hands stop shaking. Cirrus steadied himself against a wall and enjoyed the brew. After a few sips of coffee, the man's voice returned.

"Nice morning, isn't it?" It was Mr. Smiley himself again, and this time with a small paper bag of food.

Cirrus looked straight ahead toward the traffic. "I suppose," he said.

The man leaned against the wall beside Jacobs, opening his bag of breakfast. "Thanks again, man. Boy, I was starving!"

Cirrus continued sipping coffee, keeping the conversation to a minimum. "No problem." This tactic didn't work. The man's words seemed genuine and seeing him eat his breakfast made Cirrus happy. While he looked rather dirty and untidy, he ate quite politely, smiling the whole time. Halfway through his cup of coffee, Cirrus let his back slide down the wall and took a seat. After checking that it was a dry part of the sidewalk, the man did the same.

"My name is Robert," he said. "But people call me Gravity."

"I'm Cirrus."

"Good to meet ya," he said. Cirrus waited several minutes before asking him the burning question. The one reply the man must have gotten every time he introduced himself, the one he waited for. Cirrus could tell he was waiting for him to ask, too. Cirrus let him sweat it out while he finished up his food. Finally he gave in.

"So why do people call you Gravity?"

The man smiled. "Because I can levitate," he said. "Well, I aspire to levitate."

"Is that right?" Cirrus exclaimed through a smile, trying not to sound sarcastic.

"You aspire to levitate?"

"That's right," Gravity said. "Maybe if I concentrate hard enough, one day I'll be able to lift myself right off of the ground. No shit."

Cirrus only smiled in response. Actually to him, it didn't sound like such a bad idea. Besides who was he to judge? Cirrus was the guy who was looking for a real doorway to an imagined place he called Paradoxum.

"It's a spiritual thing, man," Gravity added. "You know."

"If it's something that you feel, then who am I to argue?"

Gravity smiled again, as if they had shared an inside joke. Cirrus finished his coffee and stood to continue his search for the day. Gravity stood alongside him, looking from top to bottom. His eyes paused at two spots, Cirrus's backpack and his shoes. Jacobs only stood there expressionless, letting him figure it out.

"You got a place to stay man?" Gravity said.

"No."

He looked around, mumbling his words. "You don't look like one of us."

"One of you?" Cirrus replied.

"Yeah, you know, a bum. A vagrant. Homeless."

"I haven't been for long."

Gravity smiled. "I can tell." The tone of his voice sounded like he might've offered the breakfast money back if he had known, but after a long pause he said, "You got somewhere to be?"

"Not really, not right now."

"C'mon then, let's take a walk. I'll show you around."

Since as of late, Cirrus had been involved in the walking business anyway, he strapped on his backpack and willingly followed without any questions. Like Jake the dog, Cirrus Jacobs's second road companion led the way down the rainy streets with a smile.

Lightning crashed in the distance.

*   *   *

They walked together for a brief period in silence. Cirrus watched the action taking place on the streets as he zigzagged through the obstacles. His new friend Gravity seemed to know his way around because he walked in a manner like there was somewhere important he had to be, and only he knew the quickest way to get there. Cirrus's shoes soaked up the rain that had gathered along the sidewalk surface. The soles absorbed pools of water and then spat them back out again. This repeated itself every time he took a step.

The business world was now back at full throttle. Cars, taxicabs, and buses stood gridlocked in traffic. The sound of horns and car engines filled the space between buildings. Hundreds of people walked alongside Cirrus and his new friend Gravity, some turning their noses up as they passed. They paid more attention to Gravity than they did to him, most likely due to their differences in appearance. Gravity's tale was written clearly on his back, Cirrus's was hidden within his mind.

He walked ahead, waving at people and momentarily stopping to utter phrases into the wind. Cirrus followed, undeterred by his communication with invisible people.

"Come this way," Gravity beckoned, leading him down a back alleyway.

Delivery trucks drove in and out of the narrow space between the commercial buildings. As a truck approached closely, Gravity stood aside to prevent being run over; Cirrus on the other hand, had less of an impulse. It was his pull toward Paradoxum that prevented him from moving. At the last minute in the wake of the truck horn, he too shifted out of the way. Gravity smiled all the while.

Cirrus decided immediately that he liked Gravity. It must have been his continuous smiling, unlike Cirrus, whose gloomy expression was constant. As they walked, Gravity stopped at nearly every garbage and recycling bin they passed.

"There's good stuff in these things sometimes," he let Cirrus know.

Jacobs maintained silence and patiently waited as Gravity shuffled through the contents of the bins.

"See," he said. "This is all right." He retrieved an old sweater from one of the containers and held it up for inspection. "Yup, looks all right." Cirrus noticed it had holes, but only a few small ones. Gravity neatly folded and tucked it under one of his arms. "How come you ain't looking?" Gravity asked.

"I'm okay," he replied. "I don't need any more clothes."

"There's more than clothes in here sometimes, brother. I've found sellable items. I've even found money, you name it," Gravity answered, his body jammed halfway into a bin. Cirrus listened to him talk, inhaling the city air.

Cirrus thought about why he was actually where he was. The state of homelessness was the only method of searching for a doorway to Paradoxum. He felt forced to sever the ties of his previous life because he hadn't known where his journey would take him, or how long he would be gone. He'd only begun his search, and the streets were the first place he came across to begin his exploration. Cirrus never intended on becoming a permanent fixture there, or anywhere. It was important for people to know that.

"Don't kid yourself," a familiar voice said.

Cirrus wasn't surprised to hear the voice, as he had been expecting Nimbus to return sooner or later. Keeping an eye on Gravity rummaging through the bins, Cirrus spoke to Nimbus internally. "What do you want?"

"Stop lying to yourself," he answered. "Let's face it; you're out here on the streets because you're weak. You're here because you're a failure, and you dragged me along with you."

"Quiet down," Cirrus said. "I've heard it all before. Jesus, it's like a broken record with you."

"You don't have anything, and instead of doing something about it, you do what you've always done: run away."

Nimbus's voice was beginning to make him angry. He focused on putting him away. Cirrus clenched his jaw. "Go back to sleep."

"I go when I decide, not when you want me to," Nimbus said.

"What do you want from me?" Cirrus shouted aloud, mistaking the realms of his mind with the reality of the street.

"What are you talking about?" Gravity questioned, popping his head up from a recycling bin with a puzzled look on his face. Ashamed to be caught talking to himself, Cirrus tried to respond with a logical explanation.

"Sorry, not you," Cirrus said. "I was talking to a guy down the alley who was staring at me." Gravity gazed down the lane not seeing anybody and shot Jacobs a questioning look. "He's gone now," Cirrus responded.

"Don't let 'em get to ya. Some of them can't seem to understand that we all can't have perfect lives."

"I know," Cirrus said. Nimbus's venomous voice had faded away, leaving Cirrus feeling ashamed of letting him seep into his reality. He could almost feel Nimbus laughing.

Gravity accepted this explanation and motioned for his friend to continue following. "Up here's a real good spot. Gotta get there at the right time, though, before the other boys get to it," he exclaimed.

Gravity led the way to the back entrance of a tall, slender building. Cirrus stood at its base and let his eyes follow the concrete wall up to the sky. At its peak was a giant white sign reading: *Ambassador Hotel*. They entered the backside of the building lot, which appeared to be the loading dock. There were several bins and a cardboard compacter located in the corner. Near the employee entrance doors sat a man, cigarette dangling from the corner of his mouth. He wore a standard issue kitchen uniform. Black and white checkered pants, white shirt, and a white apron. A pair of orange rubber gloves was tucked in the ties of his apron. The hotel dishwasher.

He sat on a chair, focused within the pages of a small paperback novel, unaware of the smoke trailing into his left retina.

Gravity greeted him through a smile. "Hey, Rodney."

"Hey, buddy," the dishwasher replied.

"The boys already been by this morning, I see," Gravity said. The dishwasher lowered his book, exposing the black lines of several tattoos engraved on the dark skin of his forearms. He looked toward Gravity, and then shot Cirrus a look.

"Sorry, fellas, I'm just starting a shift. If there's nothing there, then they must have come by already."

"This is my new pal, Cirrus," Gravity explained, pointing a finger in Cirrus's direction as he opened the bins to have a look. Jacobs gave a subtle nod. The dishwasher returned the wordless gesture, and then reached into his pocket to pull out a tattered five-dollar bill.

"This is all I've got, but you can get yourselves a couple of coffees with it," Rodney said.

Gravity took the money with a smile, offering Rodney the dishwasher a handshake in return. Rodney neatly placed a bookmark between the pages of his book and flicked his cigarette butt into the slushy streets. When he spoke, the last of the smoke blew through his nostrils.

"You boys take care."

Gravity waved goodbye and turned to Cirrus with the money stretched between his fingers, smiling wider than ever. "Wow, man, five bucks!"

Cirrus insisted he keep the money as they strolled further on their way. As they walked, Gravity began to further explain the daily earnings that could be gained at the Ambassador Hotel.

"You see, after the last of the staff goes home for the night," he began. "They put out all of the day's empty pop, beer, and wine bottles. Some mornings if the other boys get here first, they take everything, and sometimes, you get lucky. I've taken away over fifty dollars' worth of beer bottles before! Can you believe that? They were so heavy, I had to drag them behind me for ten blocks. I remember that day, man, was it hot!"

This last sentence was accompanied by a hearty shot to Cirrus's arm. He continued to tell his story. "The dishwashers even go in and get you some plastic bags to haul them away in, if you ask nice enough. Every one of them smokes, so there's always at least one out here. Yeah, Rodney is all right. He's given me a few bucks here and there, but mostly change and cigarettes. He doesn't talk too much, that's the other thing. I've sat there and talked to him during his entire lunch break and he only nods his head and smokes cigarettes, one after the other, until his break is over, without a single word. Maybe only to say goodbye. That's kind of weird, don't you think?"

He turned to Cirrus for his thoughts on the whole thing. Jacobs stopped midstride and gave him a turn, smiled, and nodded without a word.

"Very funny, buddy," Gravity joked. "Very funny."

*   *   *

The two new friends walked and checked garbage cans and recycling bins until night fell. Cirrus helped carry bottles and cans to the recycling depot six times during the entire day. Each time, the clerk wordlessly handed them the deposit money and continued sorting the bottles until the next time they returned. They ran into most of the same street people throughout the day who also depended on bottle returns for some extra money. Their interactions were always kept to a minimum. In total, he helped Gravity rake in twenty dollars. Not bad, he supposed. Gravity offered to split the money, since he had helped him drag it in, but Cirrus declined.

They stopped at a small shop where Cirrus bought them a large pizza to share for dinner. Gravity ate heartily, as Cirrus might've eaten bacon or whipped cream when he was a teenager. He had only spent the money he had on food so far, except for the shoe money he gave to Ms. Edgewater for Charlie. Cirrus always kept around two hundred dollars in loose bills in his front pocket, and the rest tucked in his wallet. When he paid for the food, he handed an extra twenty to Gravity in exchange for not asking any questions about it. Gravity accepted and continued eating, adhering to the rules of their barter.

Cirrus let him talk throughout the night without any interruptions, knowing he rarely found an ear to listen to his tales. They walked randomly through the downtown core, scoping out areas they would hit the next day for recyclables. Gravity told him of his life and how he had ended up in the city from back east.

"I held various jobs," Gravity said, "including a short stint on a fishing boat, some construction laboring, and even a position as a sous chef for a fancy restaurant at one point." Cirrus smiled in response. He didn't know how many of Gravity's stories he could believe, but it didn't matter to him that much. He was sure Gravity appreciated someone who'd listen, and so he listened with sincere interest. Gravity stopped to ask a question. "Tell me something about yourself."

Instead of answering, Jacobs encouraged him to continue with his own tales. "I'm just passing through," he said. "I don't really have much of a story to tell."

"Do you mind if I buy a little something from here with the money you gave me?" Gravity asked.

"No, you can do whatever you want with that," he replied. Cirrus had already assumed that this would probably be coming soon. A few blocks back, he'd had the feeling that he was being led in a specific direction. Cirrus followed without question, taking in the panorama of the buildings. They stood at the entrance of a liquor store, its bright neon sign beckoning patrons to come in and spend. "I'll wait around the corner," Cirrus told him. "Meet me over there."

Gravity went in with an almost embarrassed expression on his face, skin red from the cold. Cirrus's hands were throbbing from the freezing temperatures. The air that night was drier than it had been during the last few days. Although he sure didn't mind being dry for a change, the chill of the air made him wish for snow. It always seemed to feel warmer.

"Jesus," Gravity said as he turned the corner. "It's a cold one tonight, hey, buddy? I picked up something that'll warm us up though, don't you worry, Cirrus, my friend!"

In his hand he held a large bottle wrapped in brown paper bag.

"What's that?" Cirrus nodded at it.

"That, my friend, is a bottle of whiskey. Not top shelf, of course, but it gets the job done. Keep us warm for tonight anyway." He crookedly grinned, waiting for approval. Cirrus shrugged his shoulders and continued to walk. Gravity walked past, once again taking the role of city guide. "I know where we can rest for a while."

Cirrus couldn't say that he was surprised, but he was saddened for Gravity. A man who was able to constantly smile even in his shoes, was a man who was worthy to be king. A crown would suitably replace the dingy fisherman cap that he wore on his head.

Cirrus had once believed that he himself was capable of being the embodiment of greatness, of being a king. That was before the darkness found him. All hope of those things had left him long ago. He walked, staring at his feet which throbbed in pain from all the walking he had been doing those last few days.

They trod in silence on the streets, which had now faded from asphalt into cobblestone roadways. This was an ancient part of the city, where many of the original buildings and streets remained intact. They called it Gas Town, and it was at the end of the infamous Hastings Street.

It had long ago been converted to a tourist-friendly area where the storefronts consisted only of restaurants, bars, and shops where you could buy expensive souvenirs to send home on your travels. A few hotels, where solitary doormen could be seen in their uniforms and black caps, waiting at attention for the next customers' cabs to pull up. A phony smile waited on their faces at the ready beneath the resentment of having to open up doors and carry luggage for the rich.

Because Christmas had recently passed, the city was quiet. Most of the guests had returned home and now the lonely doorman was forced to wait until the next flurry of visitors arrived for the celebration of the New Year. One of them watched as the two homeless men crossed the street, his hands crossed military style behind his back.

"It's nice and quiet down in this part, we can rest down here," Gravity pointed. He led the way, breathing heavily from the cold. Close to the inlet, the sound of water could be heard louder with each step closer. They reached yet another alleyway just off of the main street. The bars and restaurants across the street looked to be busy that night. Patrons in their windows paid the two no attention as they ducked into the back street and sat against the brick walls. The concrete was cold at first, but eventually they adjusted. Gravity removed the paper bag and twisted the cap on the bottle. From inside the bag, he retrieved two small plastic cups. Cirrus watched as he poured two glassfuls.

"There you go," Gravity said. "Merry Christmas."

"Salute."

They took a shot of the first drink and Gravity immediately refilled their drinking vessels, pausing to inhale an aroma of whiskey before he downed another. Trying to initiate a conversation to pass the hours away, he asked questions between sips.

"So where did you work?"

Cirrus took a moment to let the burning of the alcohol penetrate into his throat before he answered. It was bitter at first, but soon became warm and comfortable. He could feel it calming his nerves instantly.

"I worked at a recycling plant for ten years," he finally answered. Gravity turned toward Jacobs and waited for him to elaborate. Cirrus began to recount some of the details of his menial job, while Gravity listened with intent, sipping at his drink to stay warm.

"I started working there when I was twenty-five," Cirrus said. "Soon after I'd lost the house to bankruptcy. I had been working full-time as soon I finished high school, to help my grandmother with the bills. Because I was an adult when she passed, I was ineligible for any support, whether it was for financial help with the house, or funding for school. I felt like I was still a child at twenty-five, and I couldn't seem to maintain a good plan of money management at the time. Since I had worked full-time, I was also denied for a full student loan, so I'd taken the first decent job that came my way."

Cirrus took a deep breath and continued, closing his eyes to recall the memory. "I had wanted to pursue a career in photography during that period, daydreaming about traveling the world with nothing but a notebook and a camera for the rest of my life. Hope. That's what it was, Gravity, and it didn't last long.

"I ended up landing a job at a recycling plant sorting the waste products that came in from collectors, businesses, and residential curbsides. They were brought in mixed and thrown on a conveyor belt, where they were sorted accordingly. That was where I fit in."

Jacobs looked over to Gravity who was listening silently with his eyes half open. Cirrus smiled, and then continued, as if he were telling a bedtime story. "Such a filthy place it was, full of giant rats and insects. It is impossible to try and describe the stench inside that plant during the summer season. We were required to be suited up from head to toe with safety gear. It was hot. After so many years at the same job, that is what I remember most: that it was hot. Nothing else. Not the people, not the work itself, and definitely not the pay. But I stayed there, sifting monotonously through garbage for ten years in all. I can't begin to tell of all the strange items that had passed along the conveyor line during my tenure," he said.

"Anything one could think of that would be mistakenly tossed in the recycling bin instead of the garbage cans, money and drugs included. While I was there, seven people in total had to be rushed to the emergency room because they had been accidentally stuck with hypodermic needles. I tried to look for other jobs, but was faced with the same type of menial work without any formal education. By the time I had been there five years, the money that was paid to me exceeded a starting wage at any other type of laboring job. That, and the fact I had subconsciously given up hope for something better in my life."

Cirrus Jacobs had succumbed to his own life of routine where, as long as the rent was paid, everything was satisfactory. Most of the people he worked with held on to the same type of attitudes. Middle-aged men who did nothing more for recreation than to drink a couple of beers and smoke a couple of joints during the weekend. When Cirrus quit, nobody made much of a fuss. He'd had some friends there, sure, but none that would understand his reasons for leaving. They were the content. Cirrus relayed all of this information to his new friend Gravity.

They had been slowly sipping on the whiskey and he hadn't noticed how much they'd finished until he glanced over and saw Gravity passed out with but an ounce or two still swirling around the bottom of the bottle. The night air had turned the last remaining shots of the brown liquid ice cold. Cirrus didn't know how much of his story Gravity had heard before he fell asleep. No matter, Cirrus's head was fuzzy and he didn't know how much of it was actually coherent to begin with.

He stood and steadied himself against the brick wall of the alley, stumbling to keep from falling over. Cirrus's legs were numb, probably due to the combination of walking, drinking, and the cold. From the backpack he retrieved his blanket and placed it over Gravity's body as he breathed steadily into the quiet alleyway. Cirrus's fingers brushed past the camera in the bag and he removed it to take a picture of him before tossing the bag aside and huddling next to Gravity for the night.

They were clear out of site, and the only thing he craved now was sleep. A strange thought passed in his head as he drifted away. He was hoping perhaps Gravity would show him his attempt at levitating.

More than that, Cirrus was hoping he might actually be successful.

*   *   *

The bartender announced last call and George mumbled out one last order for a glass. The putrid smell of stale booze lingered from his breath. George Gibson sat at their usual table, swaying on his seat and trying to remain conscious. His friends joked and laughed next to him, already used to his narcoleptic bouts after he'd consumed a dozen or so pints of beer. His girlfriend, who had broken up with him two weeks before Christmas, was also there.

Lisa Wren used to actually think that George would be the man she would marry. Now as she looked over him barely able to muster out a sentence, she wondered how she could've been so mistaken.

A few doors down from their bar slept two homeless men, both of whom fell asleep hoping they would make it to the morning without freezing to death.

"It's almost closing time, guys, you know the routine," said the waitress. "Time to get your buddy up and outta here." She said this with her eyes locked on the group, but while pointing at George.

"All right, all right, Sue," Ben laughed. "Get your ass up, Georgie boy, it's closing time." He nudged his friend of twenty years in the side. George only sat and continued to sway, his head nestled in his forearms. "I don't wanna go yet," he slurred. "There's still plenty of beer to drink."

"I think you've had enough, son," the bartender shouted from his counter.

Ben placed his hands up as if in surrender, "Don't worry, Bill, we got him."

Lisa had been ready to go an hour ago. In fact, she didn't even want to come out that night, but her friend Stacey begged and pleaded with her. They had been friends since elementary school and she would've done anything for her, except maybe this. It was hard enough to run into George around the neighborhood, but now she actually had to come out for drinks? Just because Ben hung around George, and Stacey was dating Ben, it meant that Lisa was invited to fill the odd-man-out position.

George was a big man, and even worse, an angry one. He fought strangers for pure entertainment and would get excited just getting ready to go out; knowing he planned on fighting someone at the bar. Usually it didn't matter who it was, so long as it was somebody other than Ben. They had fought on a few occasions, but Ben knew George never gave his all; if he did, then Ben might've had his nose broken several times. Everybody had a talent; George's was fighting.

"Well, we're going to get going now," said Lisa as she pulled on Stacey's arm. "It's getting late."

Stacey had realized Lisa was uncomfortable and began to stand unwillingly. She leaned across the table past George's drunken stupor and kissed Ben long and hard on the lips. His mouth tasted like alcohol. "You coming over later?"

"I don't know, Stacey," he said. "I've got to get this bastard home. I'll call you, how's that?"

She nodded disapprovingly at George. "I guess."

They walked out of the bar as Stacey took a last glance at her man, feeling glad George wasn't the one she'd had the bad luck to end up with. Lisa was glad to just be getting out of there.

"Come on, partner," Ben said as he hoisted his friend up from the chair. "You okay to walk or what?"

"I'm fine," George replied. He opened his eyes wide and feigned sobriety to convince his friend to get his hands off him. Ben let go immediately. The music faded away and the house lights began to come up as Ben and George strolled through the exit doors, soon after the girls had left. They were some of the last to leave the bar.

Outside, Ben tightened his scarf and zipped his jacket up. His friend was in no mood to do either. He simply looked down the streets for any more partygoers they might be able to connect with. The streets were empty. Most people had chosen to stay in due to the black ice conditions reported on the local weather channel. George let out a deep burp. The sound of it repulsed Ben.

He had been a loyal friend to George since the second grade, but he wondered how a girl like Lisa could've seen anything chivalrous about George. The devotion to his longtime friend would always remain intact, yet he still wondered what attracted women to such an oaf. The resentment toward George always dissipated when held in contrast to their longevity as friends. It was true that he was a bit of a brute; still, he had his good qualities. Deep down, Ben knew George had a heart. He also knew most of the aggression came from his old man, and George couldn't be blamed for that.

"I can't believe her," George muttered.

"Believe who?"

"Lisa, who else?"

"What about her?" Ben asked.

"You know, Benny, showing up wearing that tight dress," George slurred. "And then telling me that we're through. She knows she wants to get back together with me. You'll see, Benny, my man!" Ben only nodded his head in laughter as he listened to his friend pour his heart out. "I miss her, man."

Not knowing the right thing to say, Ben only continued to nod and listen, thinking about his own girlfriend. She would be close to home by now, he thought. Ben couldn't wait to get his friend home so he could go and see Stacey, if she was still up. He'd get home by two-thirty and would call.

George stumbled into an alleyway. "Hey, man, I got to take a leak."

Ben followed to make sure George didn't pass out; hanging back enough to make sure he didn't catch a glimpse of something he didn't care to see. George felt his way through the darkness with the aid of the brick wall. His level of intoxication had doubled since leaving the bar and now his throat burned for more. George stumbled haphazardly into the filthy alleyway. His shoe stopped on something. Ben watched intently from the entrance to the narrow roadway, rubbing his hands together. He kept an eye on his friend while he wished for George to hurry up.

George crouched slowly to the level of the obstacle that blocked his path. His field of vision showed a double image and he concentrated to maintain focus. The breath of the two men who lay sleeping was barely noticeable in the frigid surroundings. One slept with his fisherman's cap pulled over his face, and the other lay upright against the wall. George leaned in to get a closer look.

"What are you doing?" Ben shouted.

George turned back toward the two men, a finger over his lips. "Shhhhhh."

He examined the face of the man without the hat. He looked young, maybe in his mid thirties. He'd probably put up a good fight too, George thought. A dark beard shadowed his face, but his eyelids were reflected in the glow of the streetlights. George could see he was fast asleep. The waft of alcohol rose from the two men and penetrated George's already red nose. Couple of no good bums, George thought. From the light of the street Ben looked on, wondering what his friend was up to. He began walking toward the scene until he was close enough to see what George had found.

"Did you take a leak yet?" he asked, looking at his watch.

"Look what I found."

"What, a couple of guys sleeping in the alley?"

"That's right," George smiled.

Ben approached the three men. "So what?"

"So what?" George turned to his friend. "Let's roll these guys, man."

"For what? They didn't do anything."

George began to feel his anger rising. Who did these bums think they were? His grandfather fought and died in the Second World War; his father had served in the military too, but he was lucky enough to make it home. They had both worked hard their entire lives to raise their families. George's father *still* worked hard. He hated his shitty construction job too, but he still did it. Why should these guys do nothing and live off his hard-earned dollar? No good bums, he thought.

And Ben, he was no better. George had always hated the fact that Ben would always want to back down from a good brawl. George made sure he did anyway, even resorting to tossing a guy toward his friend during some of their altercations, just to test Ben's loyalty. Ben could hold his own, but was never willing to do so unless he was forced to. That's what George was there for.

"C'mon, man, let's get outta here. Stacey's waiting for me!" Ben said.

George's anger grew deeper. *No good bums*, he thought. He stood upright, leaned back against Ben, and suddenly kicked one of the homeless men in the chest. Ben tried to hold him back from doing so, but was a split second too late.

The man opened his eyes instantly and let out a deep breath of surprise. Panic swept over Ben like a drug, blurring the images he saw unfolding before him. The man with the fishing cap awoke at the noise and George pounced on him, throwing oaken fists against the man's face. His hat was knocked off and he screamed in pain as he absorbed the punches.

Ben stood amidst the confusion. George continued to pummel the man like a madman, unaware of his strength and unaware of the damage he inflicted. He turned to Ben and stared, letting him know what to do without a word. Ben went to work on the other, who was now hunched over clutching his chest. He hit the man harder than he had ever hit anyone before, aiming for the man's kidneys, but sending an occasional shot to his face.

Ben's head was consumed with anger. Not for the two men, but for his friend. His shoulders became sore as he bore down on the defenseless man, all the while thinking how much he hated George for putting him in that situation. Instead of his friend, he put his strength into the homeless man. George had now lost all control and had begun to tear at the fisherman's hair, hollering at the top of his lungs. Ben pulled him off and the man dropped like a rotted oak tree. The other lay unconscious against a garbage bin.

"Let's get out of here, George!"

In a drunken state of confusion, George answered back, catching his breath. "We will. First let's see what he's got. He owes us something for all the years he's been stealing from us."

"What are you talking about?" Ben screamed. George offered only silence as he turned Ben's victim over and searched his back pocket. Ben looked down the alley for any witnesses.

"You got anything, huh, asshole?" George asked the unconscious man. "Yeah, you got something."

He opened the wallet and fished out a thick fold of cash. "Holy shit, man, this guy's loaded," he told Ben in surprise. "Probably stole it."

As their attention was focused on the thief, the fisherman suddenly sprang to life. He ran hurriedly past the two and vanished into the darkness of the street before Ben and George even had their heads turned.

"Shit, man," Ben whispered. "I see the lights of a cop car. Let's go."

"All right, man, relax." George said. "Jesus."

He stood and held the man's head in his giant hands. George spoke into his ear although he could clearly see the man was still out cold. "Don't you say a fucking word, you hear me, bum?"

"He's knocked out, man, let's go!"

In a last statement, as if to show his raw power over the man, George pounded the homeless man's head into the side of the garbage bin as hard as he could, just in case he decided to wake up and talk to the cops.

Ben pulled George by the arm and dragged him into the street where they, too, like the fisherman, disappeared into the night. George had never felt more sober and he ran with a grin on his face and a wad of cash in his pocket. Ben ran faster than George. While he did, there was a single thought in his mind. He hadn't ever recalled seeing that much blood before in his life. It had stained his hands.

The police missed the two young men running as they drove by their usual route. To them, nothing seemed to be out of the ordinary that night. It was just after the holidays and most people were staying at home, they thought. That was good, because they didn't feel like getting out of their car. It was too cold.

Cirrus Jacobs, seeker of Paradoxum, lay face down on the concrete, hidden from view. His friend Gravity was nowhere to be seen, as if he were swallowed up by the night. The police officers didn't notice anything out of the ordinary. Nobody did. In the alleyway, only the rats noticed Cirrus as they slithered out of their hiding places to investigate the possibility of food, once the awful noises and bright lights had stopped.

They crept closer, sniffing the still man and drooling in anticipation of his taste.

Part II

The Road to Rebirth

Chapter Six

It had long ago become their tradition to take some time out at the end of each day to spend together. After putting Julia to bed, Emily Porter walked onto the patio to join her husband on the swing chair. The night sky was crystal clear and the brilliance of the stars filled Raymond and Emily Porter's eyes. The Doppler Effect of car motors cut through the relative silence that hung in the chilly winter atmosphere.

Raymond's legs lay outstretched along the length of the wooden bench, as he held his wife's body in his lap. He clasped his arms around her waist, holding her warm hands in his. Their lungs whispered oxygen in perfect synchronicity. This was how Raymond was so sure he was where he was supposed to be, in the grand scheme of things. She was his connection. They listened to the soothing sound of stillness, listening only for their daughter. She slept restfully in her nursery.

"What are you thinking about, Ray?" she asked.

He thought about the uncertainty of the upcoming move. Raymond Porter knew he would be unable to sleep that night. It was something he had suffered with since he was a child. Nothing out of the ordinary, just an average case of chronic insomnia. It always occurred with the anticipation of some sort of upcoming change. He remembered back to his childhood, when even something as insignificant as sports day at school would have him sleepless for days. At the time of his teenage years, days before final exams. And into his adulthood, before the dreaded job interview. Emily knew nothing of this, as he never complained about his tortured nights. Sometimes even, when he was able to get to some sleep, nightmares would plague his psyche. They were usually composed of unsystematic images that were weaved together in random sequence, making little or no sense at all. This, too, was kept from her knowledge. He felt no reason to worry Emily about this insignificant part of his personality.

Most of their family had come over the last two days, helping them to pack. No one spent more time there than her parents. They brought food and wine and the rest of his in-laws, nieces and nephews included. It was one of the most enjoyable holidays Raymond could remember. The house was filled with laughter, food, and drink.

The ambience didn't get quiet until that day, when they had to finish packing, and the reality of their departure lingered into the good time. He supposed most of them were there to spend as much time with Julia as they could before they left. Unless they came to the west coast to visit, most of them would miss three years of little Julia Porter's development. Raymond wished he hadn't taken the job offer now. He also wished both of his parents were still alive to see their granddaughter grow, as his in-laws had been lucky enough to be. His mother Dana was able to at least see the birth of her only grandchild before the cancer took her a few months later.

That was something, he thought. It was what he had held on to. Raymond remembered walking into the room during the first few weeks after the birth of their daughter and seeing little Julia nestled in her grandmother's arms, sleeping as gentle as a sunset. He was so high-strung then, so naïve. Ray's every movement was frazzled and hurried, worrying every second for the safety of his little girl. He moved into fatherhood with some struggle, but after some practice from both Julia and Emily, he learned to breathe. The birth of Julia had finally helped Raymond grow into the man he always knew he was. From the beginning, Emily thought her husband made a wonderful father, and so did Julia. And that was all that mattered.

He had walked into the nursery and witnessed his mother holding the child, exposing her eyes to the view through the outside window. It was late summer, and nothing but blues, greens, and whites filled Julia's vision. She watched quietly, blinking slowly and absorbing the panorama with her tiny pupils. His mother hadn't noticed him leaning against the doorway either, and he slipped out before she could, not wanting to disturb a precious moment. Perhaps an unseen family heirloom was being passed from grandmother to granddaughter during that moment. He had never seen anything quite like it before, not until he saw the same light between Emily and Julia as their bond between mother and daughter flourished. He learned to be calm soon after witnessing the amount of love that was given to his daughter's life, and the amount of love given at his mother's death.

"What are you thinking about, Ray?" Emily said, her question ringing in his mind.

"Nothing, baby, nothing at all."

"You sure? You're quiet," Emily whispered.

"Just enjoying the night, that's all." He squeezed warmth into her hands. "Are you cold?"

"I'm fine, Ray," she smiled. "I don't want to be anywhere else."

*   *   *

The next morning brought darkened clouds and frigid air; it was the first absence of sunshine in several days. A heavy wind swirled through the neighborhood, howling its way through the trees and over cars. The pets of their suburban environment hid behind their doors, trembling at the sound of distant thunder. Even the fish that swam in their tanks lay dormant near the bottom. Raymond lay sleepless in his bed, listening to Emily's breath as she slept. Julia, too, had decided to sleep in a little later than usual.

He had tossed the covers aside, finding it too hot to sleep, making sure he didn't inadvertently push aside Emily's share as well. When he did sleep during short intervals, the night was filled with terrors as he had anticipated. Nothing really too surprising, he thought, just some more of the randomness he had gotten accustomed to over the years.

His latest one seemed to have the same inexplicable theme, which revolved around war. The subject matter had been a recurrence since he was a teenager. They were always the most vivid of all of his dreams. Raymond found the issue quite curious since neither he nor any of his family members besides his father had served in the military. He thought about enlisting once when he was eighteen, but this notion turned out to be short-lived once word came around of his father's MIA status. His mind quickly changed. He had accepted his father's absence and understood what it meant to go off to war.

Robert Porter, Raymond's father, returned home safely after a few short months and lived a happy life with his family until he passed on three years later of natural causes. Because he had suffered no personal loss and thus no impending trauma to war, Ray came to believe that maybe he was a soldier in one of his previous existences. It might've been why those images kept returning to his dreams. Perhaps Raymond's subconscious had been regurgitating repressed memories from his distant past. He realized it was quite a ludicrous idea, yet he came up with no other explanations other than the fact his father had been missing for a short period. After discussing it with some of his closest friends, they had suggested that maybe he liked the genre and was fascinated by old wartime movies and books. Although he agreed that it sounded like a good rationalization, he knew it wasn't true. His dreams, they were too real sometimes. His latest, like most of the others, was so completely strange it made his head spin trying to figure it out.

Among several comrades, he made his escape from some sort of prison camp, ducking enemy fire with every step. Choppers hovered in slow motion, firing massive machine guns from the open hatches. The sounds of twisting metal and screaming men ripped through the landscape. The images moved fast and blurry and the whole world seemed grey, as if a child had brushed a stroke across a canvas with watercolor paint. Oftentimes, he was the only escapee who made it out of the enemy perimeter in one piece. In some dreams, Raymond had woken up just before he felt the pierce of a bullet into his chest.

The dream then took a strange twist in scenery as Raymond found himself running down the street, looking for his house and beloved family, still dressed in tattered army fatigues. There, the child took another watercolor stroke and the perception of the earth became a bright yellow, as if perhaps the closer he ran toward his home, the brighter and cleaner the world became. Instead of the sky being filled with darkness as he had witnessed at the prison camp, it had now become composed of sunshine and warmth. Raymond always caught sight of his house at the end of the street, but always woke up before he could reach the front steps, before he could see if his family had survived the world painted in grey that he had escaped.

He lay in bed, pondering these thoughts, and trying to make sense of them. Raymond listened for Julia in the adjacent room, instead hearing the wind and thunder push outside the window. Many things raced through his mind that morning. He felt the intense pressure of responsibility bearing down on his back, pushing him into the ground. Ray hoped for everything. He hoped he was making the right decision about their move, and he hoped he didn't let his wife down on his commitment to the family.

Naturally, Emily Porter knew nothing of this. He kept it hidden from her in a way only an Oscar-winning actor could. His practice should have earned him a nomination years ago. From the moment they started dating to their marriage, and even when Julia was born, Raymond paid careful attention to what he let his wife know about his inner self. Ray didn't do this with any bad intentions; in fact, his motives were quite honorable. Raymond Porter considered these emotions as weaknesses to his persona and he would never let her see that side of him. He was her protector, her shield to the world. If he were to let her down, he would never forgive himself. All of the victories he worked toward were for Emily and Julia. All of his defeats went unnoticed by them, because he buried them.

On the day of the birth of his daughter, Raymond had to excuse himself from the family to use the washroom. Once inside and alone he wept to himself, unable to control the overwhelming emotion he felt at this joyous occasion. He knew it was a natural thing to do, but felt like those kinds of things were better dealt with alone. He bore the weight of these sentiments for himself and his wife.

Emily Porter lay in bed with her eyes closed, listening to her husband struggle with rest. She rested somewhere between sleep and consciousness, knowing intuitively that he was at unrest. She felt him toss and turn, adjusting the blankets carefully so as not to disturb her. Emily had known about Raymond's insomnia since the first time they had shared a bed together. She had also known he kept things to himself when he felt threatened. Emily let him believe she didn't know, because that was what he wanted. She knew about many things, including the trip he made to the bathroom when Julia was born. It was hard for a wife not to notice her husband enter the room, swollen-eyed and red-cheeked. The rest of the family was too busy looking at the new baby, but she noticed. Emily knew he was too strong and proud to let his wife see him cry, and she admired him for it. It made her feel protected, like he had always made her feel. It was then she was convinced beyond a shadow of a doubt what kind of father he would make.

Last but not least, Emily Porter knew about his sleepless nights. She could always feel him breathing heavily, and on rare occasions, he would swing his fists against invisible phantoms during the night. She would always rub the back of his neck and send him back toward sleep. Strangely, Raymond would never speak to her about his nightmares. Emily figured that if he wanted to talk about them, he would have mentioned it to her on his own. She tried to initiate conversations that would naturally flow toward this topic but Ray never took the bait. Emily gave up this practice years ago, knowing his pride stood in the way of him speaking about these things. She knew Raymond considered these matters insignificant, even though they quite worried her at times.

"Are you okay, babe?" she asked, her voice raspy and sweet.

"Yeah, Em, I didn't know you were up."

"I wasn't," she answered. He leaned across with a smile and looked into her half-open eyes. When Ray kissed her on the lips, she kept her mouth closed, hiding an obvious smile. This was how he had always woken her up, with a kiss. Every morning she would keep her lips sealed shut; afraid her morning breath would make good grounds for a divorce. Unable to resist, he would do it anyway knowing she was too perfect to have bad morning breath. He was never wrong. He laughed, as he did every day when she did this and instantly forgot about the nightmare that had burdened his mind only a few moments before. Emily had a way of doing that.

"Are you ready for today?" Emily asked her husband.

"I suppose," he responded with a hoarse voice. "I didn't really sleep much last night. I think I was just overwhelmed about making sure everything was ready to go. I seem to have the feeling that I forgot something."

"There's nothing you forgot, Ray, relax. We'll be all right, baby. All you need to worry about today is what you're going to cook us for breakfast."

He laughed and pushed himself out of bed. "A giant stack of pancakes with whipped cream and a side of bacon, how does that sound?" She only grinned in response.

"I think I hear Julia waking up anyway, you stay in bed."

Emily Porter continued smiling and pulled the covers over her head, ready to fall back asleep for a few short moments. Raymond laughed to himself, knowing the doorbell would ring at any moment with the family arriving to see them off.

"You know what I was thinking about this morning?"

"What?" she asked.

"I guess the thought of us moving again reminded me of our first apartment. Seems like an eternity ago, do you remember that place?"

"That old grungy apartment, how could I forget it?" Emily squinted her eyes, as if trying to picture it in her mind. "Jesus, nothing ever worked in that place. I remember you having to fix something nearly every single day," she laughed. "I can still remember the horrible sound the tap made every time we had to wash the dishes, sounded like a freight train."

"Yeah," Raymond chuckled. "But that place meant a whole lot to me despite its shortcomings. It symbolized something for me."

"And what might that have been?"

"It's a little hard to explain. Well, let's put it this way, that apartment helped me to solidify the fact that you were going to be my wife one day." Emily's ears perked up and her eyes opened wider. It was a story she had never heard in the ten years they had been together. She leaned closer, maybe even a little suspiciously.

"Yeah? And how's that?" she smiled.

"Obviously you know I had dated many girls before you …"

"Many?" Emily interrupted, still smiling.

"No, not many, but you know what I mean." Ray tried to backpedal, tickled by his wife's jealousy. "But I knew you were the one because you were willing to stay with me even in that shitty old apartment. That's real love."

"Real love?" she joked. "Who ever said anything about real love?"

"I'm serious, I knew it then. You always heard about couples in the old days, like in the generation of our parents, and even our grandparents, about how they started out with nothing but each other …" Raymond lay back down next to his wife and crossed his arms behind his neck. He stared into the ceiling as if his narration was directed toward the sky. His thoughts of the restless night were beginning to fade behind him. Emily rested on one side and laid her head onto his chest. She closed her eyes as she listened.

"You know, I knew there would come a day when I would make some kind of a success for myself, and I knew my future wife and I would build that life together from nothing. I felt that those days of people who genuinely loved each other were over. It seemed women only wanted what men already came with, not what they might have become. Do you understand, Em? When you were willing to be with me despite your parents hating me at the time—and despite the fact I didn't have a car, or any money, even a good job—I knew you were the one. What's that they say, love can conquer all?"

"Being cheesy has never been your forte."

"Ha!" he smiled. "But it's true. I wanted to be successful for you. I knew you were the rare person I had been looking for."

"My parents never hated you," she slipped in.

"Maybe hate is a strong word, but they sure as hell didn't accept me into the family with open arms."

"They were just being protective."

"I know, baby," he said. "I'm just saying it was rare to meet someone who understood me the way you did, that's all. Something I can look back on now, I just thank God I was never promoted to fry guy, I might have still been there."

She laughed at this and pushed him. He laughed, too, and made his way toward the bedroom door. "You better get as much rest as you can, Emily, they'll be here soon."

"Who?" she joked from beneath the covers.

"You know who." The ringing of the doorbell drowned out the last of his sentence. Julia simultaneously began to whimper from her crib. "It's time to get ready to go, Em. I'll get the baby, you go get the door. I can't see them before my coffee, you know the rules."

"Do I have to?" she mumbled, wrapping herself even tighter within the blankets.

"Yes, baby, it's a big day."

The doorbell rang again.

Chapter Seven

"Well, well," Nimbus said. "Look where you've ended up, my friend. I could've told you your future and saved you the trouble. I knew where you were headed right from the beginning, but you were too stubborn to ask, weren't you, Cirrus? Mr. Intelligence you are, you've always known it, too. Too fucking smart for your own good. Well, my boy, where has it gotten you? Helpless and bleeding, that's where. Alone in the middle of an abandoned park, dying. You should have listened to your old friend Nimbus; you might not have ended up in this mess. Now, it's too late.

"Lucky for me, all you can do is sit there and listen. You are unable to shut me out this time, and now it is time for me to speak uninterrupted. How does the blood in your mouth taste? I'm curious; my existence is without senses, only observations. I have to assume and dream your sensory perceptions. I have so longed to taste, touch, smell, and breathe. You have denied me all of this, pushing my back against the wall. I don't even know where to begin, my boy, and I can't tell you how long I have waited for this day.

"Don't get me wrong, Cirrus, I am not without empathy for your pain; after all, I feel it, too. Just not in a physical way like you do—mine is limited to emotion. Who do you think harnesses the whirlwind inside your mind? Me, that's who. When your heart sinks in your chest, it is me who holds it from falling to the ground completely. Do you think I have not suffered alongside you? For a guy with such a profound sense of logic and reason, you don't seem to be very perceptive. You know that, my boy? I've heard people tell you you're smart, so where are your smarts now, Cirrus? Where are they?

"I must admit … I quite like this freedom. No interruption from you makes for a much better experience. I am here to help, to guide you through. I am not an enemy, merely a force for you to utilize. I have some news for you too, Cirrus: I do not sleep. Since the first day we were formally introduced to each other, I have never slept. I merely maintain my silence by choice. Everyone has a series of inner voices, pointing in different directions. It is what makes you human, to be able to make both rational and moral choices; it is what separates you from other species on this planet. Your uniqueness lies in the fact that you have the ability to audibly hear my voice, and even communicate, to communicate with me. You should consider yourself quite lucky. This, of course, is not the first case in history, you realize. They have a name for this phenomenon … the word *lunacy* comes to mind.

"Some have listened to the directions given by their voices and begin to do as they're told. Some of them even commit heinous crimes, using pleas of insanity as defense. I'm here for no such thing, Cirrus. I am here to guide you in safety. Put your trust in me, that's what I've told you since the beginning. If something should happen to you, it will surely happen to me. True, you possess the skill to put me away for the time being. But I do not sleep. I am not ignorant to the events that take place around you.

"I know what you were thinking in the alleyway when the truck was coming toward you. I felt your impulse. It is me who pushed you aside. You must understand what I'm trying to say to you, what I am trying to do for you. Do you hear me? Why do you insist on ignoring every single suggestion I make? Do you not trust me?"

"Not one bit," Cirrus choked out.

"Finally, you have awoken, my boy. It's good to hear your voice. I was afraid you were fading."

Cirrus said, "I'm not going anywhere. My body is without strength and the only will I have right now is to clear some things up with you. I lay alone and helpless, true, but there's always enough fight in me to take care of you."

"Every day our connection begins to divide a little more," Nimbus said. "I thought perhaps I was already speaking to a corpse. We share our intellect and I know that if you die, then I die. So it is my job to keep you alive. I can feel that your eyes are barely open. I can feel the throbbing of pain in your head, the hunger and dehydration as well as your loneliness. But you are alive, my boy. That's the good news."

"Alive?" he responded. "What do you know about life, Nimbus? You hide away from it, letting me deal with the pain. You lie about sharing it with me. You are nothing but a coward who shields himself from pain by hiding behind me. Never have I felt your presence during the trying times in my life, only afterwards when you come out to gloat, to tell me you told me so."

"But I did tell you so," Nimbus said.

"Fuck you. What about those things that were completely out of my hands? What did you tell me then?"

"Why do you not listen, Cirrus? You could have had a good life, if only you had listened. Tell me, why?"

"Because I refuse to lie down and accept routine."

"What is wrong with that? Would you have ended up homeless and dying? You would rather take this life than that one? What is so difficult about accepting this so-called dreaded state of routine? There is honor in that and, more importantly, safety."

"Not if you deny yourself of your own potential," Cirrus said. "Although you live there, you do not understand the creative mind. You understand neither hope nor happiness. Sacrifices have to be made for the real truths in life. I am not willing to live by a standard in which I go to the same unfulfilling job every day of my life only to die alone and empty. My mind needs challenge and stimulation like food. I need family. What you don't seem to get into your head is that I have failed on so many attempts. I understand the things I am capable of, but I can't keep from stumbling at every turn. When I was a child, I was fascinated by nature and simplicity. My infant eyes encountered and observed beauty at every turn. When people told me I could be anything I wanted to be, I actually fucking believed them! I believed these things until I was faced with the actuality that these things were simply untrue. I couldn't be anything I wanted to be without support. What are any of us without some help? Nobody has been there to help me, Nimbus. Now the connection I used to feel with my environment has been severed. I do not see beauty in anything anymore. I can't help it either. I want to see it again so badly, but I can't. That is my reality. I'm tired ... my place is not here."

"What are you suggesting?" Nimbus said.

"Moving."

"To where," he chuckled. "Paradoxum?"

"Yes. I am fully aware of my circumstances and I've dealt with them. There's no one to blame for my afflictions nor have I ever wanted someone to claim responsibility for them. It's just a lifelong case of bad luck, Nimbus. I have accepted it as my destiny. I have been waiting for an opportunity to shine through, even the tiniest hint of one, without a trace. I've worked for better things, you know. I get close, but never finish the race. The only shred of family I've had has been taken. Education has been denied to me and in turn, career. I have been deprived of any sort of intellectual or emotional fulfillment. And love, well, that's another story all together. It, too, has hidden from my reach. Do you not understand someone wanting to fight for a better existence? I am not a goddamned sheep, and therefore I cannot follow without question. I am worth something, and the simple truth is, I cannot find my way. I'm tired, Nimbus, that's all. Is that so hard to understand?"

"Love? You have dabbled in this matter," Nimbus said. "It has not been denied to you."

"Once and that, too, has left me, like everything else. I'm not saying that I have never tasted happiness, but its time far outweighs my grief."

"Boo-fucking-hoo Cirrus. And so you plan on leaving to find these things in Paradoxum, is that it? How are you going to get there? Do you think one can just book a flight?"

"There is a road, and it leads to a doorway. Of that I am certain."

"Now even I, who lives in your mind," Nimbus said, "am beginning to lose faith in your sanity."

Cirrus focused. "It has nothing to do with you. *She* lives there and I have to find her. If I can't be with her here, then that is the only other place we can be united. She is the only trace of beauty I can see; she is my flashlight, my only hope."

"Stop feeling sorry for yourself and fight a little harder. Surely you have enough energy left to do that, Cirrus."

"I have had no option other than to fight since birth so don't you tell me any different! I know in my heart I have tried, but it has been long enough. So what if I hang on here a little longer? How long then, forever? My patience has grown thin. I feel like an old man."

"Do you think you are the only one in this world with problems?" Nimbus screamed. "Stop your arrogance, my boy, it does not look good on you."

"You are the one who is arrogant and ignorant. You claim to feel as I feel, to know what I know. But you seem to ask a lot of questions. I find that curious."

"I can access only a fragment of your thought process," Nimbus said, lowering the volume of his voice. "Your decisions are not mine alone. There are many of us. I am the only one who speaks to you. When you have a thought how many nerves fire in your brain? Hundreds of thousands, millions; that's how many. When you are at a crossroads, how do you decide which way to go? You harness all of your insight. Your experience and your memory are awakened. Logic, reason, and morality are questioned. I am a part of your conscience, your confidant. I do not ever know for sure if my guidance is correct. I am here to merely suggest. You seldom listen though. And what of others' suffering? Why are you such a special case?"

"I am not ignorant to the suffering of others, quite the opposite. My torment for others is more intense than you can fathom. More than most people. If it were not true, then things such as murder, war, poverty, and starvation would be eradicated. Only a handful of people care about what's going on elsewhere in the world. They are like me, able to feel. This sensation is a burden as well as a gift. I cannot find a way to help anybody, much less myself. I don't know what to do about anything because my mind is so exhausted and I've come to an end. The only logical path I can come up with is escape."

"Do you think things are any better where you plan on going?"

"They have to be," Cirrus said.

"And what of the darkness, the mist?"

"I hope to leave those things behind. You must trust me and stand aside or be trampled. Neither you nor anyone else can convince me to stay. This decision was made after a lifetime of consideration and you can only accept this. Now leave me. I need my rest. I will resume my search when my legs have regained their strength. Until then, I have some thinking to do."

"You are making the wrong choice, Cirrus, reflect on your life and learn from those events. It's not too late for you, my boy. Go home and live out a routine existence if that's what it takes. At least you won't end up creeping toward death alone in a park like you are now."

"What makes you so sure? I am not afraid of death, if that's what you're suggesting. When it comes, it comes. There's no stopping fate. I would rather take my chances on the street to find what I'm looking for. If you're in there with the rest of my decision makers, then I suggest you have a conversation with my instinct. He might teach you a thing or two. And for your information, that last thing that'll stop me are a couple of soulless drunks looking for easy targets in the night. I have conquered much tougher adversities in my life, you know that. They can kick until my skull splits open; I'll still get up. When I go, it's on my terms. Do you understand that?"

Nimbus paused for a moment. "Understood."

"Then leave me, Nimbus, I need my rest."

"We shall talk again."

"I'm sure it's inevitable," Cirrus Jacobs said. "Now go back to sleep."

"I do not sleep, Cirrus."

"Regardless, just go away for now and give me some peace."

"Before I go for now, I must say one last thing," Nimbus said. "There is a connection still established, but you need to look through a different angle, my boy. You need to open. There are more things going on around you than you realize, things that may go unseen if you look with the wrong set of eyes. I will do as you ask and leave, but heed my advice, Cirrus. Wherever you go there will always be darkness, it is inescapable.

Like me, the darkness never sleeps."

Chapter Eight

For two full days Cirrus Jacobs lived at the park without food or water, barely conscious. He didn't even know how he managed to crawl his way there in the first place. Eyes filled with blood, Cirrus gathered up what belongings he had and felt his way out of the alleyway and back to the suburbs. He didn't remember many details, only that it was extremely cold. By the time he'd reached the park, the blood seeping out of his body had congealed into something of a partially frozen mess. The sounds of the world faded and only the ringing in his ears and the pain in his head existed. His hands hadn't stopped shaking since.

The drunken thieves had stolen all but $187 from Cirrus. They must have made off with close to $2,500. If they had checked his front pockets they would've stolen it all, every last penny. Not that it mattered to Cirrus really. It was the fact they had stolen money from someone they fully understood to be underprivileged, and it was what had upset him more than anything. The natural law of karma was something that none of us could outrun. It lived on the earth and in the air. Those two young men would get what was coming to them, of that Cirrus was sure.

It wasn't himself he was much concerned about. It was Gravity, and he had no idea of his whereabouts or his condition. The tattered fisherman's cap was the only trace left behind by him. The last Cirrus could recall, Gravity was being beaten on by the bigger of the two. When he advanced on Cirrus, Gravity took off running. He was glad Gravity got away, although he worried in his frail state, he might've been quite badly injured. As thin as he was, Cirrus was sure Gravity must have at least broken a bone.

As for Cirrus, he'd been laying there on the stage putting on an exciting show for all his invisible fans for two days, unmoved. The adrenaline in his body pushed him far enough to reach the park, and then left him there to rot away on the stage. He had virtually no memory of getting there at all, only what he could piece together.

He awoke for the first time when daylight pierced through his eyelids. He shuffled further into the darkness of the backstage area in response. His mind was completely disoriented and he thought he might've stayed awake for only a few minutes that first day. Every part of his body was in severe pain. He lay face down on the old wooden platform inhaling dust, body flattened out against the corner. Cirrus could feel the blood trickling from his split lip and could only see out of one eye as the other had swollen to titanic proportions. Initially he thought his ribs had been broken in several places; luckily, they were only bruised during his ordeal. Also, he had lost a tooth.

He assumed that he must have slept for nearly a full forty-eight hours and when he came to the second day; the pain had subsided to half the intensity. The loosened tooth was the first thing he felt when he awoke before the rest of the pain set in and the only energy he had left in his body was to work it out of his mouth by pushing on it with his tongue. The feeling of it hanging on by a thin thread of gum was more than he could bear. He spat it out of his mouth and watched it roll along the floor before it fell off the edge. Cirrus thought about his invisible audience sitting in front of the stage. *How was that for a show, folks?*

Curiously, hunger hadn't affected him much, unlike thirst, which had been scratching at his throat since he regained consciousness. He could hear his stomach growling loudly, although he'd had no hunger pains. When Cirrus had the energy, he crawled to the edge of the stage and drank handfuls of snow. At that moment, he wished he had a shot of Gravity's whiskey, anything to stop the pain.

It was early morning of the third day of his recovery, if that was the word you wanted to use. Very dark still, and quiet, too. The day before New Year's Eve. He'd been thinking quite a bit about making his way out of the city and was just waiting until his body had healed enough to allow the journey. Otherwise, he would have ventured out the night after he'd met Gravity.

After Cirrus had placed the blanket over his body and leaned against the wall to catch his own sleep, he had felt Paradoxum's energy. It was an unexplainable instinct, and more of a physical sensation. It almost pulled him right out of the alleyway. A second impulse, stronger, kept him there; he felt that perhaps it was a premonition of the events to occur a few minutes later. If he had not been there next to his friend, Gravity might've had to endure the violence of the two men alone, and it could've killed him. They would have double-teamed him and as thin as he was…well, Cirrus didn't want to think about that.

As painful as the physical had been, Cirrus's mind had suffered tenfold. It was a dark and pounding hurt suffered internally, not to mention the vague memories of conversations he'd shared with Nimbus. The fragments of the last conversation he could recall were quite longer and more intense than any of their previous quarrels. Cirrus had the feeling his weakness gave Nimbus more strength. Something was said about succumbing to routine, that much he did remember.

There was no sign of either one of his friends in the animal kingdom either. Neither Jake the dog nor the white owl had returned to the park. The first of his recovery nights as he passed in and out of consciousness, Cirrus vaguely recalled an animal of some sort sniffing around the area, trying to draw nearer. He wished he knew if it was Jake or not.

His energy that night had returned quite sufficiently and all he was doing now was waiting for the full daylight so that he could venture into the city and buy himself some food. It was like the pain drizzled out of his spine like a black, viscous fluid. Cirrus could feel the fuel deficiency quite profoundly. Strolling through the city with a bruised and battered face could look quite appalling to some people, but in all honesty, he had stopped caring. His days in the city were numbered.

*   *   *

Fresh fruit. Funny how even in the dead of winter one could still obtain the ripest and tastiest fruit the world had to offer. He stood in a small market filling his basket, trying to blend in with the rest of the crowd. They tried not to stare, but they couldn't help themselves. His cut and battered face could not be hidden away and the void left in his mouth by the missing tooth was impossible to conceal. He carried on his way without care, let them look. It meant nothing to him anymore.

He had what he needed, two large bottles of water and a bag of fresh fruit. Cirrus Jacobs left them staring behind him, just as he had left his former life.

BING! BING! BING!

In the distance church bells rang. Their sounds went unnoticed by the people on the streets. He viciously chewed through one apple after the other, throwing the cores into every wastebasket he passed. Cirrus's mouth was forced to chew on one side as the gum where his tooth used to be had swollen. His feeding frenzy was momentarily interrupted as he stopped to look up at the sounds of the church. They came from the top of the street and cut through the traffic noise. Cirrus walked toward them, not knowing why. Intrigue, he supposed; besides, by then he had quit questioning his instinctual forces.

He reached the front steps of the church in minutes, and by the time he had gotten there, the black clouds had opened up once again. Sharp raindrops shot from the sky and at this, people on foot hurried their pace and car horns began their attacks, almost as if the event was scheduled. No one stood near the entrance of the church. People passed, but no one stopped. The last of the bells had stopped as he approached the bottom of the steps. He had never once in his life stepped foot inside of a church. Not for any particular reason, mind you; it was just one of those things. Cirrus would admit he'd always wondered. Churches fascinated him, but mostly for their architecture, nothing more.

The door was made of ancient wood and stood ten feet tall. Oversized square, brass handles replaced the doorknobs. As he opened the door, a warm wind pushed its way past him, smelling of pine, wax, and scented incense. An enormous room opened up before him past the lobby. It was dimly lit and eerily quiet. The wooden doors closed gently behind him and deafened the noises from the street. At the altar, which looked to be miles away, there were candles burning and they danced with the wind that he brought with him from the outside. Only two people accompanied him inside and they were deep in prayer at the front of the church.

As Cirrus peered in, a quiet voice blindsided him from behind. The hood of his yellow rubber raingear had blocked his peripheral vision and it wasn't until he'd had a chance to unveil himself that he could catch sight of the man speaking to him.

"Welcome, son, can I help you with something?"

The man's voice was quiet and mousy. His voice matched his appearance. A small man, about a foot shorter than Cirrus. He wore a traditional black suit and a bright white collar upon his neck. A genuine, upstanding man of the cloth. His thinning red hair was neatly combed to one side of his head and his small horn-rimmed glasses softened his appearance even further. With his hands crossed at his waist, he spoke gently. "It's a cold one out there today, yes?"

"Yes, Father," Cirrus responded, not quite sure how to address the man. "I'm Cirrus."

"Nice to meet you—Cirrus, is it?"

"Yes, sir, Cirrus Jacobs."

"I'm Father O'Connor," he said. "I haven't seen you in here before." Suddenly Cirrus felt overwhelming weariness. He assumed that all of the remaining blood in his body had rushed toward his stomach to aid in digestion. It might have been the smells inside the church. It made him feel somehow passive.

"I hope you don't mind, Father, but I just needed a place to think for a moment and I just happened to pass by the church, so I stepped in."

"Not at all, son, that's why we're here," Father O'Connor said. He placed a hand on Cirrus's shoulder and guided him further into the dimness of the stone building. "Take as much time as you need, Cirrus, all are welcome here. Don't hesitate to call if you need anything."

Father O'Connor stood at the threshold of the darkness and guided Cirrus with his hand toward the back row of pews. He stood at the end of the long walkway of carpet, staring directly into the face of an enormous sculpture of the crucified Jesus Christ. The kneelers at the front were undeterred at his presence. When he turned to face Father O'Connor, Jacobs found he had vanished. Once again, the candles flickered.

A sensation of sadness filled Cirrus. It was because yet another human being had referred to him as *son*. The first was Mr. Everett, then Ms. Edgewater at the shelter. Prior to this, he had never heard himself referred to as somebody's son. It felt both pleasant and gloomy at the same time, like a rainstorm in the middle of a beautiful summer afternoon.

He took a seat at the second to last row of pews and blended in with the darkness. The wooden seat was comfortable against his back. Cirrus's lungs inhaled the deep smells of the church and soothed his windpipe. *Why am I here? What exactly am I looking for? Was it silence from Nimbus? Like Dracula, perhaps he is unable to stand on holy ground? Not likely,* Cirrus thought.

His beliefs in those matters were rather thin. Maybe it was some kind of clichéd form of salvation he was searching for. Perhaps the simple act of stepping into a house of God would provide him with clarity. Maybe a little part of him was hoping for something like that, hoping for some kind of a miracle. At that point, Cirrus was about ready to try anything to fill the hole inside his chest.

He closed his eyes, and even they hurt. Cirrus could feel the water running off of his raincoat; it pooled on the hardwood of the bench. The stone fortress of the church amplified the murmured prayers of the devotees at the front. He couldn't make out their faces, only shadowy silhouettes behind the flickering of the candles. The ambience was looming. He was suddenly possessed by a deep yawn and his eyes closed even tighter. When he exhaled and opened them, the scenery in front of him had changed.

Back in the empty room with an open window. Paradoxum. The little girl drawing pictures at the windowsill. Cirrus in the corner, leaning against the wall amid the darkness. It was the state of his lucid dreaming. He was clearly aware that his body still rested in a darkened church, fast asleep. Although he knew he was there, he was also aware that he was here, in Paradoxum. His experience continued, as if another page had been written in his book of dreams.

Within his dream world, he crouched in the shadows of the dusty room, staring. It had been far too long since he had seen her. Her presence filled him with happiness, even though he was aware it was an artificial form of one. Slightly above the hardwood floors rose a grey mist; and it swirled around her tiny legs. Like always, she was unaware of his presence.

Cirrus opened his eyes and floated back into reality. It had been the first time in his life that he had transferred back to reality of his own accord. He had to; the pain was too much to bear that day. Being there only amplified his loneliness and that hollow feeling in his chest was much too heavy to carry. Two single tears ran down his cheeks and dripped onto the yellow rubber of his jacket. Cirrus's eyes turned beadily to the sides to reaffirm his solitude, although he made no effort in wiping the drops from his face. Again he was at the stage where his body felt robbed of all energy. It was amazing to him how much power the mind possessed, enough to alter the physical body. On the one hand, it could be harnessed into healing, and on the other, it could aid in deterioration. He felt like sleeping again.

"There is much to do today, my boy. Now is not the time to sleep."

Cirrus had wondered where Nimbus had been; he had almost started to miss him. Cirrus's back slid further down the pew, hiding even further into the shadows. His head leaned to one side, eyes unfocused onto the Jesus sculpture. Maybe it was *He* who had spoken and not Nimbus.

"We must get back to walking," Nimbus said.

"Since when do you care?" Cirrus questioned, suspicious as always.

"I don't, if you must know. I am not on board with your plans, Cirrus, but I must encourage movement nevertheless. I, too, despise standstill. Besides, I don't care for this place. It defies simple logic."

Cirrus sighed. "As much as I might tend to agree, one must respect the fact that places like these are built and are able to sustain for centuries based on simple hope. Hope is everything, Nimbus, not that I'd expect you to understand."

Nimbus inhaled, and then spoke. "Might we have a single conversation and avoid conflict for once, my dear boy? I just want to get out of here, I feel restless. We shall save our debates for another time. Today, I do not have the patience."

"Are you all right, son?" Father O'Connor suddenly said.

Not surprised, Cirrus didn't even turn to respond. "Yes, Father, I'm just leaving."

"It is not my intention to run you off. You are to take your time."

"Thanks, but I really have to get going," Cirrus said as he stood to walk away. Father O'Connor reached out for his arm.

"I must ask, what brought you here today? There must be something, son. You had said that you had never been here before. Did you mean here in particular, or to church in general?"

"I have to go, Father," Cirrus calmly stated as he walked toward the exit, leaving the question unanswered. The man of God whispered a final statement as Cirrus flooded the lobby with light from the outside landscape.

"There must have been some reason, son. You may want to put some thought into it."

The fresh air from the outside immediately began to clear his head and filled his cells with instant energy. Suddenly Cirrus didn't feel as lethargic as he did when he was inside the church. Nimbus rushed back.

"You don't need to listen to him, Cirrus. You know the next thing he was about to say was how you walked into that place because God himself guided you there. You know that, don't you?"

"I don't know anything, Nimbus."

"So you're saying that maybe the man upstairs pushed you in there?"

Cirrus began walking rapidly, gaining momentum with each step. The flash of his camera shrouded the stone architecture of the building as he snapped its picture for his collection before tucking it back into his knapsack and continuing to walk.

"Well?" Nimbus said. "Are you not going to answer?"

Cirrus offered only silence and by the time he had walked five city blocks, Nimbus had once again retired into whatever labyrinth he dwelled in. Jacobs felt his annoyance scratching at the back of his brain. It was funny to him that he continued to separate himself, when he knew that they were one in the same. The questions he asked were questions Cirrus asked himself. Perhaps though, he was too afraid of some of the answers. Nimbus at least had the strength to be aggressive; something Cirrus had always lacked.

What is it that had forced me in through the doors of the church? I don't recall ever having the need to do so in the past. The thought iced his blood. Had God actually called him through the sounds of the bells? He had given up the notion of religion long ago and rarely, if ever, gave it any thought. He supposed when one suffered loss, it became a much safer place to live if he didn't rely on someone else saving him. *I barely trust myself. How am I to trust anyone else, much less a higher being?*

The rain fell harder than before he had stepped in through the confusion of the church. Cirrus couldn't even pull up his hood because it had filled with water. No matter, really, he was actually beginning to enjoy the raindrops that day. It felt as if he was being cleansed, perhaps from someone above. Maybe today was the day he could make his peace with God, if he did indeed exist on some higher level. To Cirrus, it felt like a final goodbye, though. He had the eerie sense it would be the one and only time they'd have the chance to communicate. The only hope for another encounter with God and dear old Cirrus Jacobs was perhaps left for Paradoxum.

He walked deeper into the city and it seemed once again he was pulled into a place he didn't intend on stepping into. It was like he was physically dragged in through the doorway as he hurried past. This time, it was a place he was familiar with and was quite fond of.

This was his church, the place he had always come to for spiritual guidance. A maze of shelves and books always put a smile on his face, even that day, battered and bruised and soaked from the freezing rain. Even the air smelled of knowledge. Strands of pearls woven together in an infinite state. The downtown branch of the Vancouver Public Library.

He had decided it would be his final destination in the city before he ventured off into the uncertainty of the rest of the world. It was the one decision he had made as of late that could have been deemed concrete. That place had always been the foundation of what he considered to be his home. The backbone of his city. Cirrus found it peculiar that one was able to actually fall in love with the concrete, steel, and glass of his city. To him, the trees were exactly where he would have put them. The rivers snaked through the landscape in perfection. And the buildings were just tall enough. Not too slender and not too wide. They were big enough to declare themselves worthy competitors for a world-renowned city, but were not so tall as to loom over its inhabitants and cast fear into visitors. The concrete monoliths were spaced apart enough to allow air to move about and not trap filth within the city, both as a tangible term and as an abstract one. The only flaw in this design was unintentional, Cirrus was sure. When the money flowed within a city, the less fortunate were pushed out, as he had encountered in the streets earlier. From there at the main library, those dark streets seemed a continent away. In reality, they were just a few city blocks.

The downtown branch of the library was built with the intention of encapsulating the coliseums of ancient Greece. In the center you could look straight up into an infinity of books and information. People swarmed around him in traffic formation. They were like the rapids of a raging river and Cirrus was a rock in the center of the riverbed. The waters parted and flowed around him to continue their path toward the ocean. No one stopped to glance at the toothless man standing in awe at the simple sight of books. No one cared to acknowledge the rock who acted as an obstacle to their pathway.

The ceiling was so high that he wished he could fly to get to the top floor where they kept the reference books. Maybe he would close his eyes and float right up there, arms outstretched, like maybe Gravity would have done if he could indeed levitate as he so wished. Cirrus could relate to his affinity for flight. He closed his eyes and concentrated, but was still left feeling the ground beneath his feet. Sadly, he would have to take the stairs.

The path over each step had been carefully outlined since Cirrus always started at the same destination whenever he came there. The top floor was always skipped, unless he had reference questions to look up, and his journey always began at the second-to-top floor where they kept the recordings. It was quite a collection if one actually took some time to look through them. It was their composition of classical works that kept Cirrus coming back. Movie scores, actually, the ones they put out in addition to the soundtracks.

Soundtracks were filled with the songs for a movie; the score was the symphonic music one heard in the background. For Cirrus, the right background in a movie could make or break a scene. Those recordings were often difficult to find in music stores, so he'd been coming to the library to sample them for years. If he liked them, then he'd order them. Sometimes he played the scenes from the movie back in his head when he listened to them, and sometimes he let the music create new scenes in his mind. He supposed it was the creative part in him. The need to fuse pictures with words or music.

The library had a section with headphones and couches and Cirrus thanked God, because that day the area was empty. The downtown library was so big that only rarely did he run into the same staff day after day. They were mostly students who worked part-time in between exams and so it seemed there was a constant revolving door of people flowing through. He didn't want to speak to anyone he knew. They would surely be asking what had happened to him and since he hadn't even seen himself in a few days, he wouldn't know how to answer. Cirrus had the feeling that maybe he looked much worse than he actually felt. He had already noticed the infectious smell seeping from his broken tooth.

The discs were listed in alphabetical order and he pulled exactly the one he knew he wanted to hear that particular day. It was the original score to the motion picture *The Truman Show*, composed by Burkhard Dallwitz and Philip Glass. The main character's instincts in the movie, like Cirrus's, guided him to explore out into the unknown. It was why Cirrus liked it so much.

Jacobs placed the headphones over his head and selected repeat for track seventeen. It was a song called "Truman Sets Sail," his favorite on the score. Before he leaned back on the couch, he snapped a picture of the ambience swirling around him. None of the patrons seemed to notice. A member of the staff did and came rushing over, pointing his finger as he approached. By the time he reached the couch, Cirrus's camera was safely tucked back into the knapsack. A grey mane of long hair was tied back in a messy ponytail behind the librarian's neck. His expression looked to be of a man who had nothing better to do with his time than to try and enforce meaningless rules to make himself feel important in the world. He squinted his eyes at Cirrus through thick, black-framed spectacles. As he walked over, his stomach heaved from side to side.

"Hey, you can't take pictures in here!"

Cirrus gave him a smile, minus a single tooth, and in its place only a bloodied gum. Not the kind of smile one would consider friendly either. The librarian understood the point instantly and made one last statement before passing without stopping.

"Just no more, sir."

Cirrus watched him pass with his peripheral vision and settled back into the chair as the song began. Instantaneously, the scene in front of him slowed to a sloth's pace. Like a scene out of a movie, overexposed with a misty haze. He closed his eyes and let the music fill his ears … fill the hole in his chest. The sounds made him feel as if he was actually levitating, like he had wanted to do only moments ago. If he opened his eyes he would surely fall back to earth, and this was something he was not willing to do just yet, thinking he'd float above the couch for a little longer.

One day, perhaps you will get the chance to hear this song for yourself. You could feel what Cirrus felt on that dark winter morning before he'd leave his city forever. Maybe then he would feel as if someone was with him, listening to the same thing he was listening to, and feeling how he was feeling, even if you were a world away. There would at least be some spark of a connection.

Maybe then, his loneliness wouldn't be so agonizing.

Chapter Nine

Raymond Porter's Volkswagen coasted smoothly down Highway 1 toward the west coast. He changed gears in ecstasy, happy to finally be on the road. Driving had always been one of his greatest pleasures. The sound of the motor filled him with satisfaction. Julia sat in the back strapped carefully in her car seat, doing what she spent most of her time doing, sleeping gently. Raymond's wife Emily, also tired, leaned her head up against the window, trying to keep her eyes open.

Although the weather was fairly dark that afternoon, her perception was viewed through dark sunglasses. It was an attempt to conceal her swollen eyes from the crying she had been doing earlier that morning. Her mind processed infinite amounts of data as her eyes scanned the landscape, trying to keep up with the speed of the car. With one hand she gripped the door handle, with the other, she caressed Raymond's neck. She had been doing this for so many years that sometimes Raymond felt strange when he drove by himself. Unable to feel her security beside him, he would have to remind himself that she wasn't there.

The trees and rocks of the highway side raced by in a blurred frenzy. Emily kept her eyes low to the ground, following the contours of the asphalt. When she wasn't doing this, she was following what was going on in the sky, searching for any birds that would be gliding past. She, too, enjoyed the sounds of the motor. Raymond's voice penetrated through the sounds of the engine and the wind.

"Are you still tired?"

"How could I not be, Raymond?" she whispered, throat still raspy from emotional wear. "Don't get me wrong, I love the family, but Jesus, it takes a lot out of me having to say goodbye to all of them."

Raymond took her hand from his neck and gave it a soft kiss. His mind edited his thoughts and responses, knowing that by telling her everything would be all right, he would be stating the obvious. Ray understood that she already knew this, and gave her the silence and the time she needed to deal with things. Meaningless and clichéd terms wouldn't work. At the moment he couldn't do much to help her feel better; besides, he felt solely responsible.

Little Julia yawned in the backseat as Ray watched her from the rearview mirror.

"She seems all right with everything," he said, nodding in Julia's direction. Emily turned to look at the baby and rubbed her hand across Julia's forehead.

"I wish things could still be so simple, Ray."

"They're not as complicated as they feel, Em," he said. "It's just that everything is occurring so fast. You'll see, when we get there we'll be so busy getting settled in, we won't even notice. I won't start work for another month, and by then, I'm sure you'll be ready to get back yourself."

He picked up her hand once again. "Don't worry, I'll take care of us. You have to trust me."

"I do, Ray, it's still hard," she sniffled.

He attempted to change the subject. "Are you excited about seeing your friends again?"

"Actually, yes, Carol says she's coming over the second we pull up."

"Carol, my God, I haven't seen her in years. What is she doing these days?"

"She works for the phone company there," Emily said. "Says that maybe she can get me a job, too. The money is good, but the hours are all over. We'll have to figure something out, Ray."

"A minor glitch in the system, Em," he said. "Maybe Carol can babysit."

"Yeah, right. She's a busy single girl. Do you think she's going to want to spend her weekends watching a baby?"

"Oh, come on, babe," he joked. "That little angel in the back, who wouldn't want to spend every waking moment with her?"

Emily gave him a pity laugh for his sarcasm. "Ray, pull over at that next exit. I need a cup of coffee." At Emily's request, he turned the wheel to the right, thinking to himself that maybe a cup of coffee sounded good. They had only been on the road for eight hours, and making good time; but he knew the journey wouldn't be rushed. He had been looking forward to enjoying the ride through the country.

Raymond had spent the morning loading their belongings with the courier company while Emily entertained the family and finished up the last of the cleaning. Since they would be back in three years, Emily's youngest brother had volunteered to rent out the house until they returned. He was a good man and in fact had become one of Raymond's closest friends over the years. Her brother Barry was one of the people Ray let in on his strange dreams. He was a man who held the deepest respect for his sister. It was one of the reasons Ray had befriended him so easily. That, and the fact he was the funniest guy Ray had ever met. He was great with Julia, too, and that sealed the deal.

Their belongings would arrive on the west coast a day after they would. Their furniture would remain with Barry, and he would guard the house with his life, Raymond knew. Ray had carefully planned out every detail of their travels, learning from his father the discipline needed to pull off such an arduous task. They carried with them only what they needed for their travels and everything else had been shipped. At the last minute Ray had felt an impulse to switch courier companies because he felt the man they sent to do the pickup seemed like a scatterbrain. Raymond never liked such men. He himself had plenty of jobs he hated in his life, but worked himself to the bone nevertheless. He wished everyone could have the same standards as he did, the kind he learned from watching his mother.

Raymond had planned a surprise for Emily when they arrived in town, and he had found it hard trying to keep it a secret, especially when he had seen how upset she was when they left. He was on the verge of letting it slip out, but was somehow able to keep control. They had agreed to rent a small space for their tenure in the big city, and Raymond had flown out a month earlier to do some reconnaissance. While there, he had managed to secure a beautiful condo overlooking the waterfront. It was only a few hundred over their budget, but he knew it was something she would appreciate.

Emily had grown up in a small town on the east coast, where her father was a fisherman. She would often tell him stories of her childhood spent on the beaches of her hometown. Her father had switched careers when she was ten, and their new life in another town began, as far from the ocean as you could imagine. The view of the water was something he hoped would help fill the void left by her parting with the family. He had also planned on taking her furniture-shopping, and insisting she pick out anything she wanted for the new place. They would paint and hang pictures, like they did when they had moved into their first dingy apartment. All of the expenses were to be put on his credit cards, and he wouldn't give it a second's thought. When they had moved into their first apartment so long ago, he didn't even have the option. Raymond Porter had even made up quite a convincing story about how he'd had to settle on a mediocre space that was probably too small and that they would probably have to move again when the time was right. Raymond had even thrown in a couple of sympathetic apologies to further add conviction to his stories. To his amazement, she only kissed him on the forehead. He knew she was one of a kind, but he expected her to be even a little disappointed. Emily's tolerance had confused him and he wondered maybe if she'd had a few tricks up her sleeve as well. It was a fun game to play.

Now, night began to fall. They would drive as much as possible, stopping at rest areas to sleep. Raymond had insisted he do all of the driving and thought he'd only require a few hours of sleep each night to be able to drive for another day. He had estimated that it would only take about two-and-a-half days at most. Emily agreed with no resistance; knowing her husband better than anyone, she knew he was adamant in his plans. Besides, she trusted him.

They would of course, spend a few nights in motels if things became too uncomfortable, but Raymond knew most of their time would be put toward driving. It was their first trip as a family, and he wanted Julia to see the sights of their country. Ray knew that somewhere down the line, she would somehow remember the landscape her father had shown her when she was a little girl. When she was old enough, he would tell her about himself.

He would tell her about his childhood and the different towns they had lived in. When she went on her first date, Ray would tell the story of how he met her mother, and how he knew in an instant she was going to be his wife one day. When Julia went off to college, he would tell her of his own struggles, and how he gained his education through his own life's experiences before going to college himself as a mature student, realizing later in life that if he wanted to provide his family with security, he would have to do something other than punch a time-clock in a low-paying factory job day after day. If he had the courage, maybe he would even tell her about the dark family secret he had kept even from Emily until late in their relationship: that his father had been a heavy alcoholic, even violent at times. These were things he knew he would have to tell her at some point during her life, to help her understand where her parents came from. How they had managed to overcome adversities in their lives to become the people she knew. These were lessons he knew would be imperative in her journey. Raymond Porter wanted to protect his daughter at all times, but knew he would have to let her go one day to learn things on her own.

When Raymond graduated from college and landed his first important job, he had almost felt guilty. Guilty from what, he could never quite pinpoint. Maybe it was the fact that he had finally left his miserable childhood behind. It was one of those things that had always propelled him forward. Once he had attained success, it felt strange to let his past spiral behind him. Like it was one of his nightmares he had forgotten about. People would look at him differently now.

Porter had always taken pride in the fact that he had risen above and beyond what had been expected of him. Everyone who knew him also knew about his past, and they respected him for it. Now he feared people would see him as always being successful, like he had never been standing in the mud to begin with. Maybe they would think his rich parents had put him through school, and he had taken whatever courses he needed just to get by. Perhaps they would think he had never conquered adversity, or that his entire life had been a cakewalk. People would think at first glance that Ray walked with his eyes closed, and that he had stumbled upon a beautiful wife and a good job merely by luck. This was not the case, and these thoughts irritated him. They irritated Raymond because he had worked so hard for everything in his life. It was a backfire to success he had never anticipated. It was the price he had to pay.

To embrace the success he had achieved, he would have to slowly bury the worries of his past. One day, they would be buried deeper than even he could remember, but he knew he would never forget. It was what kept him grateful every morning. It was the catalyst that kept him loving his wife and daughter with the intensity he that he did.

"Are you done your coffee already?" Emily said.

"No, still working on it."

"What did you get?"

"The largest size coffee they had," he laughed. "With two extra shots of espresso."

"Jesus, Ray, your eyes are going to shoot right out of your head."

Already feeling the buzz from his beverage, Ray answered with a smile. "Yeah, I know. Can't wait either."

Emily looked toward her husband. "Something about being on the road excites you doesn't it, Ray?"

"You know, it really does. I don't know what it is either. I remember when I got my first car in high school, you know, I showed you the pictures of that junky old Toyota. The boys and I would go camping every summer, every chance we got. That was when I got the bug, I suppose. What can I say? I love this. It reminds me of those trips you and I took together when we first started dating. Just driving and not knowing where we were going, there was such an excitement in that. Nothing was planned and every turn was spontaneous."

"So what are you saying, that things have become boring?" she leaned in.

"No, not like that, Em," he said. "Something about the freedom of the highway, I guess, that's all. Things haven't gotten boring since the baby, just different. I couldn't imagine living my life without either one of you. I'm just saying, it's been a while. Besides this is our first trip as a family, did you realize that? It makes for a whole new experience all together."

Emily smiled. "Nice save, Ray."

"I know," he gloated.

"You always seem to be in a haze of such deep thought," she said. "It's nice to see you looking a bit more relaxed today."

She placed her soft hand once again on his neck. A tingling ran down his spine and over his arms. "It was all the planning, Em. Now that we're finally on our way, I'm able to loosen up."

"Do you want to talk about your sleeplessness last night?" Emily asked.

"Not really, babe, what can I say? Just some strange dreams, that's all. Nothing to talk about."

"I worry about you sometimes, Raymond. I can tell they really bother you and you won't speak to me about them. Did they involve another woman?"

He turned to his wife cockeyed. "C'mon, Em, that's ridiculous. You know you're the only one for me."

"It's normal, Ray, but you could tell me if that's what it was."

"What do you mean, normal? With whom do you spend your nights?"

She turned to face out the window, smiling. "You know, who don't I dream about? Brad Pitt, Denzel, DeNiro. The usual suspects."

"You're serious?" he laughed.

"Yeah, why not?"

"Because you're married to me, that's why."

"It doesn't stop you from dreaming about Scarlett Johansson. Don't try lying about it either, Ray. I see the way you look at her."

He chuckled even harder. "So what? She has a pretty smile."

Emily held his neck a little tighter, as if she were about to choke him. "Yeah...her smile, that's why you like her."

"Honest, baby," his laughter grew in response. "I wasn't dreaming about any other women. They were all busy last night!"

Emily rolled her eyes. "Yeah, well, Denzel wasn't."

"Ouch!"

They both laughed as the car coasted a few more miles closer toward their destination. In the back seat, Julia Porter awakened to the sound of laughter. Instantly, she began to cry. Both Ray and Emily turned toward her.

"What's the matter?" Emily asked her daughter.

"Maybe she needs to be changed," suggested Raymond. "Is she hungry?"

"Ray, you watched me feed her only twenty minutes ago, have you forgotten already?"

"I'm losing my memory with old age, it's not my fault."

"She's probably unfamiliar with waking up without her mobile. It must be strange for her to wake up inside the car." Emily stroked her hand against the baby's forehead again, humming Julia's favorite song. Julia stopped crying and began to flail her arms around wildly. "Maybe I should hold her."

"I don't think it's a good idea, Emily," Raymond said. "If she's stopped crying, then she'll be fine. I'm not taking any risks unstrapping her from the car seat. If you want, I'll pull over at the next rest area."

"Well, she's stopped crying anyway."

"She's probably just bored. That's what happens with extremely intelligent babies."

"And where do you suppose that gene comes from?" Emily asked.

"There's no question, Em."

"Ha! What makes you so sure?"

"She will be a creative genius, like her old man," Raymond said. "I can feel it."

"Maybe she'll be a technical mastermind, able to process numbers easily like her mother."

"I don't see that coming from her. I think she'll paint wonderful pictures, write compelling novels, and make beautiful music. She's an artist, like me."

Emily rolled her eyes. "When was the last time you did something artistic, Raymond?"

"There's no need to hit below the belt, Em," he chuckled. "I'm going to finish writing that novel one day."

"How long has it been now?"

"I lost count after the first five years."

Emily laughed at this and was finally able to remove the sunglasses from her face, instead wiping tears of laughter from her eyes, shaking her head at her husband.

"Screw it," she said. "She'll be the leader of the free world."

"Damned right!" he responded, slapping the steering wheel with his hand. "How about some music?"

"What do you have in mind?"

Raymond thought for a moment. "How about something classical?"

"How about something a little more upbeat, like the Dixie Chicks?"

"Are you kidding me, Emily? Please, the baby is in the car, we can't subject her to that."

"What's wrong with my taste in music, Ray?" she questioned.

"Dixie Chicks? You know they say classical music better stimulates the mind. It's good to start children listening to it at an early age. They say it helps to strengthen the mind, build focus. Something about the strings helping to soothe the brainwaves."

"And where did you hear this?"

"I don't know, I read it somewhere," he said. "Probably in a magazine at the doctor's office. Anyway, it's scientific, Em, you can't argue with that."

"I'll tell you what, we'll listen to your classical for a bit and then we'll listen to my Dixie Chicks. Deal?"

"Not much of a deal, if you ask me," Raymond joked. He retrieved his CD collection from beneath the seat and slid one into the player. The sound of a deep cello radiated from the speakers, filling the space within the car with ambience. Julia paid close attention from the backseat at the wondrous sounds. "It's the score from *The Shawshank Redemption*, what do you think?"

"It's nice, Ray."

"Listen, do me a favor and open up the backpack in the backseat. I bought something for Julia when I was at the store last week. I figured I would get her started early for her training as an artist, and also keep her from getting bored during the trip. It's in the side pocket."

Emily unzipped the pack and retrieved a small pad of paper and a box of brightly colored Crayola crayons. "This was sweet of you, Ray," she said. "But I don't think she's old enough for these just yet. She'll probably just chew on them."

"Don't worry, they're nontoxic. Just give them to her and see what she does. Let her pick out a color. I think she'll choose green."

"I'm pulling for the orange," Emily said as she placed the pad on Julia's car seat table. Julia looked at the colors in wonder as her mother held the open box before her. Raymond looked on with curiosity through the rearview mirror. As he did, Julia reached for the box and placed her hand over each color before finally selecting a crayon with her left hand.

"We both lose, Ray, she chose the red one."

"Red?"

"Yeah, the candy apple red."

"What's she doing with it?" Ray asked excitedly.

"Well, she's just waving it around."

"That's a good sign; she's trying to get the feel for it."

Emily enjoyed the animated way Julia held the crayon, like she was absolutely ecstatic about her new toy. "You know what?" Emily said. "I think she's left-handed."

"Holy shit!" Ray exclaimed. "They say like 80 percent of all artists are left-handed."

"Is anyone in your family a southpaw?"

"Not that I know of."

"I wonder where she gets that from. Maybe it's too early to tell anyway, she's only waving it around."

Raymond focused his concentration back onto the highway and turned up the music. "It's pretty cool, anyway."

Emily, too, turned back to the scene in front of her, glancing back momentarily to check if Julia had tried to eat her new toy. Neither one of them noticed as Julia began to scribble lines onto the blank sheet of paper with her left hand. She moved the crayon in an unsystematic pattern while she looked out the window. It fit comfortably in her tiny hand. Raymond finally saw as he looked back.

"Look, Em, it's her very first piece of artwork. Don't let her chew on it. I'm going to frame that one for sure. I'll show it to her university professors when she gets accepted for a full art scholarship."

Emily shook her head in laughter and reached for the CD collection. Little Julia Porter looked out of the window and smiled into the starry sky, still scrawling heavy red lines onto the paper.

Through the wispy clouds, the moon smiled back.

Chapter Ten

Cirrus Jacobs floated above the couch, listening to his music in the library when a tap on the shoulder transported him back into reality. He opened his eyes with the feeling he had been in slumber for days. During the last few days, he had noticed an intense need for sleep. It seemed that the further he slid down the hole toward heavier depression, the more time he wished to spend in another world. At times, he had felt like curling right up on the sidewalk, amid all the people and rain, and just taking a nap.

As the minutes passed by, his body healed further from the assault—that is, when it had the energy to break free of the lethargic state it had fallen into. Although Cirrus was feeling better by the hour, he didn't know how much more of the side effects of healing he could stand. Since the night in the alleyway his head had been filled with aches, the kind that he had never experienced before. If Jacobs was given the choice, he would have easily chosen dealing with the physical pain rather than the pounding headaches. It was as if Nimbus was swinging a sledgehammer against the confines of his brain, attempting to break his way free. Cirrus would be happy to set him free, if only he could.

"Cirrus?"

He took off the headphones and turned to face his questioner, following the direction by way of her sweet scent. She looked different than the first time they had met. The apparent lack of confidence he had noticed the first time they met had been replaced by a strong sense of self, and it now beamed from her skin. Her blonde hair was still tied behind her neck in a ponytail, and she held an armful of books. She too, like Ms. Edgewater, looked like an angel. She spoke again, softly.

"Cirrus, is that you? Do you remember me?"

"Tara, from the shelter," he said, trying to smile without exposing the void in his mouth.

She took a seat on the opposite end of the couch. "Yes, I didn't think you'd remember. You don't mind if I sit, do you?" After a brief moment of pause and realization, she asked sympathetically, "Are you all right?"

"I'm okay," he responded. "It's not as bad as it looks."

"It looks pretty bad, Cirrus."

He had been fearful he would run into someone he knew, and he felt utterly ashamed. Darkness enveloped his mind and left cobwebs in its wake. Cirrus couldn't even muster out a single word because he had frozen. He wished he could just slither away.

"What happened?"

"I was jumped by a couple of guys, that's all. Nothing too serious."

"Have you seen a doctor?" she said.

"No, there's no need." If she really wanted to know the truth, he would've told her that he didn't care if he rotted away and left for good. It made no difference. He didn't think it was something she would have wanted to hear. "I'll be fine, Tara," he continued. "The healing is just taking some time."

"Can you even see out of your left eye? It's swollen shut. And your face, it's bruised so heavily." She could see that he wanted to change the subject as he squirmed in his seat.

"It'll be fine."

"Sorry, Cirrus, I wasn't trying to make you feel uncomfortable. I'm just worried about you, that's all."

"Thanks, but I'll be fine."

She leaned forward. "So, have you seen Ms. Edgewater recently?"

"No, I haven't been by for a few days."

"Me neither, midterm exams are coming up and I've had to study."

"What courses are you taking?" he asked, grateful for the change in subject.

She put his question aside and stood. "Can I get you a cup of coffee or something?"

"Sure," he decided. Maybe a cup of coffee would dissolve the webs inside his mind. She made for the java stand and left her belongings behind. "Be right back, sugar and cream?"

"Plenty of both thanks."

Suddenly he felt extremely hot, and could feel beads of sweat forming along his temple. The thought of just getting up and leaving occurred to him, anything to get out of the sudden heat. Cirrus carefully wrapped up the headphones and returned the CD to its place, deciding against leaving and risking being responsible for her stuff going missing, if it was the only excuse he could come up with for not leaving.

His hands had begun shaking again. Jacobs hid them inside his pockets and glanced around the floor. The scene had returned to its usual place, no more slow motion, as it had been when his perception was viewed through the music. In addition to the shaking, a lump had begun to form inside his throat. He didn't exactly know what he was so afraid of, but the realization didn't seem to help with the paranoia.

"There you go," she smiled, handing over a steaming cup.

"Thank you so much," he said, standing to receive the cup to avoid spilling and to relay his respect and gratitude. The coffee tasted good. As he sipped, he appeared as calm as still water, but on the inside he was desperately searching for suitable conversation. He didn't want to offend her, or say something weird. He was afraid Nimbus would try to stick his foot in Cirrus's mouth. "So what are you taking at school?" he finally mustered.

"I'm only taking two courses right now," she said. "It's all I can afford at a time."

"I understand."

"One of them is a standard business course, marketing and advertising mostly with lots of hands-on computer training. I'm also taking an introduction to creative writing."

"Really?"

"Yeah," she proudly smiled. "I wanted to take something I was really interested in instead of going through school with nothing fun to look forward to."

"Do you do a lot of writing?"

Cirrus found her shyness rather fitting, and the confidence in her words was without arrogance. She spoke wisely beyond her years. By way of her demeanor, Tara's intelligence seemed impossible to ignore.

"I'm new at it, but I'm trying. I'm not very good, though."

"I'm sure you're just being humble."

"Do you do anything like that?" she asked.

"No, I don't write myself, but I love books."

"I know the feeling."

"I've thought about it, but I don't think I'd be much good at it, to be honest," he said. "It's like my love for music, too; the world is a much better place because I choose to stand aside and let the experts make it. I have been taking photographs for most of my life, that's about it."

"Cool, I like photography, too. Have you ever shown your pictures?"

"In a gallery, you mean?"

She smiled. "Yeah."

"Nah," he said, starting to feel much more relaxed. "I just get them developed and put them away in a box."

"Why do you bother taking pictures if you just hide them away?"

"Just a hobby, I guess."

Her direct line of personality interrogation continued. "What do you take pictures of?"

"I don't know really, all sorts of things. Usually whatever I feel intuitively about. I carry my camera with me wherever I go and just snap away. I have it with me right now," Cirrus said. He took it out of the pack, looked through the viewfinder, and focused on her face. She shied away, looking to the right. "Do you mind?" he asked.

She only shrugged her shoulders in response and smiled. He snapped a picture as her face caught the natural light from outside the window. It cast a shadow on her left side. Instinctively and perhaps quite insanely, he wondered what she would have named her dark inner voice—if she had one.

The film inside the camera was black-and-white. When he took photographs, especially of people, he tended to stick with black-and-white-exposures. Somehow he felt that through that type of film, emotion could be seen through the paper. After all his years of taking pictures, he had never been able to put his finger on why. It just was. Landscapes were sometimes better left for color, but living creatures, as well as some inanimate objects, came across better with the greys and dark qualities of black-and-white. If one were to snap a photograph of an ancient tree with a trunk whose girth measured over thirty feet, it was possible to be able to see its life somehow contained within the picture. How long it had stood, all of the changes it had witnessed on the earth around it, as well as all of the life that it had housed within its branches. A sculpture that stood in a park, perhaps for decades, went unnoticed by some. Its stone face might be scratched and weathered by the elements over time, the green discoloration of lime seeping through its pores. The symbolism of this statue, its purpose and its meaning, could sometimes be captured on film.

The picture that he had just taken would emit these qualities when he developed them, if ever. Her bright blue eyes would show through, even within the colorless exposure, one would be able to instantly pick out the hues of her eyes. Her kindness and innocence would be portrayed without flaws, he was sure. And the subtle smile she gave would indicate her mood, maybe even the time of day. All of these things could be seen within a picture. If, as Nimbus once said to Cirrus, one looked with the right set of eyes. As per his routine, he safely tucked away the camera back in its home after it served its purpose.

"Thanks," he added. "That one is going to be great."

"So what are you doing here?" she asked, once her shyness had left.

"I thought I would stop in and take a last look before I left."

"Are you leaving town?"

"Yes, to see a friend for a while," he lied.

"I'm here just to get away and maybe try to squeeze in a little studying. My boyfriend and I split up recently and I can't stand being cooped up in the house, especially this time of year."

"I'm sorry to hear that."

"Don't be sorry, he was an asshole anyway," she laughed. Cirrus, too, couldn't help but chuckle. He was glad at least she was honest, and he couldn't help but respect her integrity. Most girls her age might've been more content moping around the house. "It wouldn't have been so bad if I hadn't been living with him," she continued. "But I had to move everything to a friend's house for now. I can't really afford my own place right now and I'm debating whether to phone my parents or not …" she stopped abruptly. "Shit. Sorry, Cirrus, I'm ranting … I didn't mean to do that. Sometimes I just forget."

He leaned a little further into his seat and sipped his coffee. "No worries, go ahead, I like to listen."

"Are you sure?"

"The floor is yours, Tara."

"Well, the thing is, I haven't spoken to them in two years."

"Two years and not even once?" he asked.

"No, the funny thing is, it was because of Steve to begin with; he's the one I was living with. They just never liked him, right from the beginning."

"Parents sometimes have that instinct with their kids."

"Were your parents like that?"

Cirrus thought about her question and reminded himself that he had no such chance for guidance, except from his grandmother, God rest her soul. She had always trusted his judgment in whatever he pursued, relationships included. "No," he said, wanting to further clarify but not feeling like lying to her again.

She accepted his one word answer and maintained the conversation. "Well, they weren't happy I moved in with him, to say the least. Our conversations slowly broke further apart until the relationship I had with them disappeared altogether."

"So they were right about Steve?"

"Yeah, but I'd never tell them that."

"I'm sure if you called, they would apologize. They sound like good people, even if maybe they went about it the wrong way. The way I look at it, they were so worried about their daughter's welfare that they forgot what they were trying to protect in the first place, in the shadow of the issue at hand. Who knows how either one of us would react in the same situation with our children."

"That's one issue I'm glad I don't have to deal with right now. I can barely take care of myself, much less any children."

"Were you in love with Steve?"

"At first I thought I was … Jesus, I can't believe I'm sitting here at the library telling my life story to a virtual stranger. I am so sorry."

"No need to apologize, Tara. All of us need someone to listen sometimes. Really, I don't mind," he said.

"Well there's nothing more to tell, really. I think I always knew what my parents were talking about, but something inside myself thought that he would change."

"He never did?"

"No," she said. "Turned out to be the asshole they always said he was."

Cirrus attempted to provide the best advice he could offer. It was amazing that a man who lay stranded somewhere so far down into depression was able to offer advice to someone else. He prayed that she was unable to see through his façade.

"Well, seems like there's only one choice right now, Tara: to go home. That's where you need to go to regroup. Don't you think?"

"I suppose," she said. "Something's stopping me, though."

"What?"

"I just know what it's like in that house. We're constantly butting heads."

"Are you the only child?"

"I have a younger brother."

"Maybe he needs you, too, Tara. The only reason you would have to consider in not going home, was if it was a bad situation; something that would jeopardize your safety."

She glanced up at him for a moment, like he had accused her parents of something. "No, Cirrus, they're very loving."

"Look, Tara," he pleaded with his hands. "I didn't mean anything by that. I'm just saying, you don't realize how important family is unless you don't have any."

Tara's eyes glanced into his with sympathy. He could tell, she now saw the truth about him in his eyes. She knew that he never had any parents. She knew he had bent the truth in the response to her question moments ago. Tara didn't bother confirming these facts, she just continued.

"Maybe. I'm still mad at them."

Cirrus nodded and sipped the remainder of his coffee, afraid to let himself become vulnerable again. It was a shame, really, that one could become afraid of the truths about himself. Tara placed her empty cup on the table and put her feet up next to it, crossing her arms behind her head.

"Have you ever been in love, Cirrus?"

He could feel the rush of blood to his face and the heat it produced. Jacobs looked up into the ceiling and tried not to let the lump in his throat give away any more secrets. "Once."

"What was it like?"

"From what I remember, it was nice." It had been his second lie to Tara, because he could remember it like it was yesterday. It was a memory he'd been trying to escape for years. The truth was he could remember even the most minute of details.

"Nice, that's it?" she said. "That's all you have to say about it?"

"It was a long time ago."

"So tell me about it."

"What do you want to know?" he asked uncomfortably, still looking into the propeller of the ceiling fans.

"What was her name?"

"Anna."

"What did she look like?"

"Do we really have to talk about this, Tara?"

"Yes, we do, Cirrus. I didn't want to spill my guts about Steve and my family, but I did anyway. Besides, what the hell else are we going to do this afternoon? I don't have any place to go, do you?"

He paused and then finally answered. "She looked like an angel, like you."

"Oh, stop," Tara joked. "Really, what was she like? I'm curious. I need a face to go with the story."

"Well, how do I describe her?"

"Close your eyes and remember."

"She was a little shorter than me, with long blonde hair. She always kept it up in a ponytail, like you do. I remember how much I loved that. I don't know what it was about it, but I loved it."

"What else?" Tara asked with interest.

"Well," he continued. "She was always smiling, that was something else that really attracted me to her. Even when things weren't going so good, maybe if she was having a bad day, her smile would never fade. It would lessen maybe, but never disappear altogether. I knew from the first instant I laid eyes upon her that I was in love. I know that sounds goofy, even to me, but it's the truth."

Tara smiled and lowered her gaze. Cirrus hadn't intended on thinking about Anna that day, but now that he had started, he felt as if he couldn't stop; like his memories were a dam on the verge of being crumbled to bits. After that perhaps, it would be an impossibility to stop all of the waters from flowing through. All of the feelings that he carried with him about her were suddenly in the forefront of his mind. He had never spoken to anyone about her, and it felt good to remember. "I have dated women in my life, but have yet to find one that makes me feel like she did. I think we both shared that sentiment."

"Go on ..." she said, head balanced in both palms. "When did you know for sure? When did you know that she felt the same way?"

"Well, we spent a great deal of time content with just being next to each other. It was like we communicated without even speaking sometimes. We had spent the day walking around the park downtown and had stopped to rest on a huge piece of driftwood that had settled on the beach ..."

As he closed his eyes to focus on the recollections to relay them to Tara, he was transported back there, onto the beach. He opened his eyes in Paradoxum as an observer to the scene of two lovers sitting on a log, his arms wrapped around her waist. Both of them faced the ocean. It was a beautiful September afternoon and the sun hung lazily in the sky. Behind the two stood a forest of trees. Cirrus, the observer, walked closer to try and feel their connection. As always in his dream world of Paradoxum, his movement went unnoticed. Even there, he wore his tattered clothes and yellow rubber raingear. Cirrus looked down at his shoes and noticed how broken they appeared to be. The energy it took to look pained him.

It was Cirrus Jacobs of the past who sat along the makeshift bench, woman nuzzled in his arms. The scene was from a time which seemed like an eternity ago, a time when there was happiness in his life. Even his appearance had not a single trace of present-day Cirrus, the way he looked as the onlooker. Cirrus of the past kept his hair neat and trimmed. He was clean-shaven and smelled of imported cologne. His eyes were neither bruised nor cut like the onlooker's, and he housed a full set of teeth inside his mouth. Cirrus, the observer, was what was left after the man in front of him had shed his skin. Anna's hair blew with the late summer breeze. Like always, a smile rested upon her face.

"We were sitting on the beach and I was holding her. When I reached around to give her a kiss, my lips tasted salt."

"She was crying?"

"I wouldn't say crying, but a tear nonetheless, even maybe just a single one. Well, I panicked of course, thinking that she had been tormented about breaking up with me and had been crying or something out of guilt."

"So what did she say?"

"She said for me not to worry about it and that she didn't want to be anywhere else. I admit that I did worry, but it was only my own insecurities I was wrestling with. I understood that like me, she had remained closed from people and she was happy to be able to open up to me. The overwhelming feeling of release is a strong force, I know because I felt the same way. Have you ever felt like no one could know you? What if one day you unexpectedly found that person? It is much to take in. She told me that without a single word. I knew it then, because I felt as she did.

"If you must know, Tara, I do not believe in God, never have as a matter of fact. But that day, when I dropped her off at home, I thanked God that I had met her. I felt a need to, like I owed him something. I remember as I drove home, thanking everything I saw in front of me. The trees and the grass. The sky and the air. Everything. And because I had never seen God, I looked for his face everywhere, just so I could say thanks. Do you believe that? That's how she made me feel."

"So what happened?" Tara said. "If you tell me she's dead, I don't think I could handle it right now, Cirrus."

He opened his eyes and once again traveled back to reality. The air of the library carried with it none of the life it had exhibited on the beach. There was a clear distinction between the two opposing realities. "No, Tara, she's not dead. Honestly, I don't know what happened. It was like our relationship started off with such intensity that it just simply burned itself out somehow. It's the only way I can explain it. What am I supposed to say? We simply disconnected somehow."

"After what you just told me, you're saying you don't know why things fell apart? How could you not?"

"I don't know, Tara," he confessed. "Some things aren't meant to be, that's all."

"That's all?"

"I don't know."

"When was the last time you saw her?"

"Over three years ago. She used to work here at the library, that's how we met. I don't know what became of her. Probably married by now. I hope that bastard treats her well."

"Why didn't you ever try finding out? It didn't bother you?"

"Of course it did," Cirrus said. "But I just couldn't bring myself to be around her. It took too much out of me. Besides, I quit asking myself why things turn out the way they do. It was the simple realization that things are the way they are. That's what happens in the world sometimes."

"That's a crazy story, Cirrus."

"I feel like throwing up."

"Really?"

"No, I'm just joking," Cirrus said.

Actually he really did feel like throwing up. He thought perhaps it had something to do with the air changeover in between dimensions. It was very strange. His experiences, they were becoming more of a real sensation by the day. Maybe it was a sign he was getting that much closer in finding his path there. In his nose, there still lingered the smell of ocean mist. *Dear God*, he thought. *Am I losing my mind?*

"So when are you leaving?"

"Leaving?"

"To see your friend?" asked Tara.

It took a moment for him to recall. "Oh, my friend. Today I think."

She stood and began to gather her things. "I should get going, Cirrus. It's getting a little late. But it was nice talking to you, really."

"Are you going to go home, I mean to your parents' place?"

"I think I just might, you've given me something to think about. I didn't expect that today, but maybe it's a good thing."

"Do you mind if I walk you home? I understand if you don't, being around a guy looking like I do can't be good. I just thought …"

"I think that would be great," she cut him off, "if you don't mind walking through the rain."

Cirrus thought she would laugh if she knew the truth, if she'd known he'd been walking in the rain constantly for nearly a week. On second thought, he was sure she could smell the rain on his clothing.

*　　*　　*

They walked for nearly an hour in the freezing rain, Cirrus with his yellow hood pulled over his head and Tara, brandishing an oversized black umbrella. They talked little during their stroll, having covered much in the way of conversation at the library. She did however tell him more about her family, mostly of the humorous tales of her younger brother. Quite a character he seemed to be, and from what she told him, quite intelligent, too. It seemed her parents had had the combined luck to produce very bright children.

At their first meeting, Cirrus would have never guessed her background based solely on looks. She seemed to be a quiet, withdrawn young girl. After their conversation that day, he realized she was quite a unique and outspoken individual. Tara was very political in her perspective of the world and even mentioned that she was involved with many groups dedicated to economic equality. Cirrus supposed it was her motivation for working at the shelter in the first place. He would admit she really surprised him and by the time they had reached her parents' house, she reminded him less of his grandmother, and more of Anna. Her interest in and knowledge of politics, economics, and philosophy made him feel refreshed. Even her interests in religious studies, he came to find, resembled his own outlook.

She made him feel like he had been mistaken in the comment he'd said to Nimbus about feeling like he was the only one who felt a need to contribute and offer change. Cirrus could tell from the energy that surrounded her, that Tara was one of those people who was absolutely essential in bringing positivity within her environment. Maybe she was one of those people who was able to see the light in any situation, even within a train wreck like him.

"This is it, Cirrus," she said, turning toward the house. "Not your typical family house."

"It's your home, Tara."

"I suppose."

They stood on the lawn of her parents' home. The front patio looked to be in the midst of renovation, a renovation that had been going on perhaps for a couple of months. The wood of the foundation was exposed and the nails that held it in place had rusted from the rain. "He started it last spring," she said, almost reading his mind.

To him, despite its unfinished construction, it still looked to be a wonderful place to grow up. Christmas lights decorated the trees and the windows. Smoke billowed from the chimney, filling the air with a comfortable, warm feeling. Through the window, her younger brother could be seen playing video games as he lay on the floor beneath the Christmas tree, his facial expression changing with each move he made on the joystick. Her father sat in an armchair, sipping a glass of red wine, engulfed in a paperback novel. Neither one of them saw Tara and Cirrus standing in the rain.

"I guess this is it, Cirrus," she said. "Thanks for listening."

"They'll be happy to see you."

She leaned forward to give him a hug goodbye. He hugged her back, but kept his distance for fear of infecting her with his griminess, or even maybe with his insanity. "Take care," she said quietly. "I'm sure we'll run into each other again, maybe at the library."

"It's a possibility," he responded. "See you soon."

The lump in his throat returned, as if he were saying goodbye to someone for the last time. Cirrus turned his back and began walking, not looking back. Once he heard the sound of the front door close, his pace doubled.

*   *   *

Cirrus Jacobs stood at the onramp of the road that lead to Highway 1, his back turned against the downtown core of his beloved city. He had thought about cutting back across town from Tara's and stopping through the park he had considered his home for the last few days. On the off-chance maybe Jake the dog had returned, Cirrus was hoping he'd be a willing participant in making the journey with him. Of course, Jake would never return, as Cirrus already knew. Night had fallen and he made one last stop for a few bags of food before he would walk to the highway, drenched in the rain.

The glow of the city lights echoed in the background. He felt too cowardly to actually turn around to say goodbye like a man, so he only stood there with his hands in his pockets and offered the sentiment internally. In front of him lay the Georgia Viaduct, and this was the road that would lead him to Highway 1. It wound its way into the horizon, and it was the way. It was the road to Paradoxum. The walk would only be a day or two at the most, and its beckoning had never felt so strong.

Darkness loomed in the sky, casting out the chance to spot any stars. As far as he could see down the roadway, ominous clouds hung low over the landscape. Although Cirrus could only hear the sounds of traffic, he could see lightning forming within those distant clouds.

He was sure as he walked toward them, the sound of thunder would be sure to follow. It was inevitable. After a deep breath, he forced himself into walking toward his imminent future. Behind him, the city carried on with its usual activities. He had to stop himself from sobbing.

The city didn't seem to care that one of its children had left forever. Cirrus didn't really know what he expected, just something. Some kind of feeling, some kind of sign that would beg him to stay. He might've reconsidered. Now he walked with the realization that the world would continue to revolve even after he'd left and entered into Paradoxum. No one would remember him and no one would care. The only traces of a life he'd left behind were a box full of records and photographs that he'd given to John Everett, his father's gold watch, and a broken tooth lying in the dirt at the foot of the old wooden stage. That was it.

As he walked along the viaduct, something to the left caught his eye. Since the city had been preparing for the upcoming winter Olympics, there were many new buildings being constructed around Vancouver. He turned to see a building he had never noticed before. Along the length of its entire roof was an oddly placed sign. In large LED lights read only one statement: "Everything is going to be all right."

Cirrus lowered his head and began to weep. His city it seemed, was indeed begging him to stay. Despite this, he kept his pace.

*   *   *

Along Highway 1, there were few cars. It was eerily quiet; as if everyone else in the city had been invited to an exclusive party, and perhaps his invitation had been misplaced in the mail. A noisy car drove by every now and again, but overall, most people had chosen to get dressed up and attend the festivities far away from the highway. Jacobs walked on the grass alongside the pavement on the embankment that supported the roadway, where no one could see. The grass was flooded with water and he almost slipped a time or two just trying to stay balanced. It was better than the alternative, which was to walk on the highway itself, and risk being hit by an oncoming car. Not surprisingly, the rain doubled its attack from the sky.

His feet ached, but he ignored them. Left. Right. Left. Right.

His pace was one he had never attempted before. He felt he had to get as far away as he could, as quickly as he could. Cirrus walked about ten miles before the road turned a corner and the cityscape vanished from his sight. It was then he'd had built enough courage needed to turn around and take one last look. The whole time he was walking, he could feel it watching him. It seemed so distant, so tragically far away. Cirrus Jacobs's head boiled inside the yellow raingear. His throat burned and his hands shook violently. His heart sank and his eyes shed tears. He wiped them away with anger and turned to walk again, fighting the impulse to sob like a child. The lump in his throat quivered with this action. Paradoxum awaited and the need to reach his destination had never felt more urgent. Had never felt more real.

*   *   *

"I see you have not changed your mind Cirrus," Nimbus said.

He began to run after he'd turned the corner on the highway, which had now snaked through the last of the suburban areas of the city before it opened up to only trees. They provided the darkness and comfort that he had now grown accustomed to. It brought a feeling of secrecy. His feet pulsated in his shoes as he jogged toward Paradoxum, like he was fleeing from a crime scene. After Cirrus had crossed the main bridge in the city, he once again retired to the edge of the embankment, where he could carry on with the business at hand, unseen.

It was the first time in his life that he had stepped foot onto the platform of the bridge. People took them for granted as they drove over them, busily making their way to their appointments. Making their way as fast as they could to meet the deadlines of their despised lives and jobs. It made no sense. Rushing to do things they didn't want to be doing in the first place, and passing by extraordinary things in the process. Unless one had stood on the bridge, one could never attain the true scope of its beauty. The view from up there was utterly breathtaking. It was a perspective Cirrus had never seen before. He even stopped to look down, and was so far up that he had to imagine what the water looked like below. He had to piece together the evidence from the sounds of its crashing waves, and the view through the mist that shrouded the base of the bridge like angry ghosts. It felt like the water was a million feet below.

Upon his return to land, he began to run. His patience to finally see the wonders of Paradoxum had grown thin. He no longer cared how he got there, so long as it was fast. Cirrus ran until he was out of breath, and then slowed his pace back down to a walk. The vapour escaped his lungs in deep billows.

The perception of time had once again left him. It felt exactly like when he had left John Everett on the front porch of their apartment complex. He walked then, unaware of the time or how many hours had passed. If someone were to ask, he would have been unable to give them a definitive answer. In the sky behind, toward the city, the lights on the horizon had disappeared. If Cirrus were to guess, he would estimate it would've taken a person many hours to make that much distance by foot. To him, it seemed that only minutes had passed and furthermore, his legs could sustain a journey of a thousand more miles. He found himself, once again, caught within the whirlwind of darkness. The pain of his legs and feet were no longer felt. The hurt in his heart did not exist and the pain in his head had mysteriously disappeared. There was only one goal, to reach his destination. He had entered once again into the place where time did not exist and the mist seemed to spring to life like bacteria.

It was the first time in his life he had actually called on Nimbus to come forward. There was no life around him and the fear of what might've been hiding within the shadows had his mind filled with fear and confusion. The trees seemed to laugh as he walked past, hunching forward with the wind. They no longer felt safe. Even the drone of cars that passed on the highway seemed to stop for too long a period. It felt as if he had walked clear off the face of the earth. There was no one, so he beckoned for the only person he could think of to help him through, to help overpower the loneliness. Nimbus came within an instant, like he knew the call would be coming, as if he were waiting.

"You seem to be in an awful rush, Cirrus," he said. "What's the matter, afraid of something?"

"Hello," Cirrus said. He tried to sound calm, although his heart raced rapidly in his chest.

"Are we feeling alone? Are you unable to outrun the darkness on your trail?"

"I just wanted someone to talk to, that's all."

"So talk, Cirrus. You never answered my question. Why have you not turned and headed toward your home? Why have you not changed your mind?"

"Because I no longer have a home, Nimbus," Jacobs said. "There is a new home for me, and I am headed in that direction."

"If you knew what lay beyond the borders of your beloved Paradoxum, you would reconsider."

"And I suppose you know?"

"Tales of what lay beyond have been discussed for centuries. Do you think you are the first to explore its realms? Do you think it is yours to take possession of? You will be in for a surprise, my dear boy." His voice had turned into a snakelike hiss, dark and brooding.

Cirrus spoke so forcefully that he thought he must have spoken aloud; it was impossible to tell. "What makes you so sure?! Who are you that you get to possess this knowledge of a place that I have created?"

"Loss of control is never an easy thing to deal with, Cirrus. You, it seems, have been slowly losing it for years. Your reign has almost come to an end and, as in all aspects of history, all leaders must eventually pass the torch of supremacy. My knowledge comes from your mind, have you forgotten? If you are unable to focus enough to gain admission, then that is no fault of mine. It lies there somewhere, every answer to every question. Perhaps that is the definition itself of insanity: being unable to access one's own mind. It will be a lonely place without you, my boy, I assure you of that, but we'll get by, I'm sure."

"You're talking nonsense," Cirrus said, focusing on the road in front of him. "You know I am at my most vulnerable, and you can't help but exploit it."

"Is that so?"

"That's right. I summoned you only to have a conversation, not to listen to another lesson."

"You will realize the truth shortly, but I will humor you for now. So tell me, Cirrus, what is it that you wish to talk about?"

A car raced past and disappeared into the distance in a flash. Cirrus didn't even hear it approaching behind him. It flew past at an incredible rate of speed and all that he could make out was its midnight blue color in the moonlight. It seemed like the only sign of life he had seen in the past four hours. He knew that couldn't be true, even there as he approached the outskirts of the country. Its presence helped to solidify his reality.

"I don't know, Nimbus," he continued. "I just need to hear a voice to pass the time. I don't know how much farther I have to travel."

"Shall we speak of Paradoxum?" Nimbus questioned.

"No, something else."

"Because I know how much farther we have to go. So do you; it seems you have forgotten, but I can remind you."

"Not now, we'll get to that. Tell me something else, something totally unrelated," Cirrus said. "What do you look like? I don't think I've ever bothered to ask."

"I don't look like anything, smart boy, I am without a body. It is something you've known since the beginning."

"If you did, what do you think you would look like?"

"I don't think that's something you would like to know."

The answer had Cirrus's curiosity piqued; it was a question that had randomly passed into his mind. He often wondered if Nimbus intentionally placed a thought process for him to discover, and then pretended like he knew nothing about it. One thing Cirrus did know for sure was that Nimbus couldn't be trusted. He wondered in how many ways he had been manipulated by his own mind. The sound of thunder echoed in the distance. The highway seemed to be empty once again.

"Sure I do," Jacobs responded. "What do you think you would look like?"

"Like you, of course, with a few modifications."

"Modifications?" Cirrus wondered.

"Yes. Naturally there would be changes between you and me."

"Changes like what?" he probed.

"You were born into this world and then you grew," Nimbus hissed. "And I grew within your mind. Imagine if I were to suddenly take shape, what would I look like? That is the question whose answer you seek? Let me tell you, my boy, it would not be pretty.

"I would look like you, but much skinnier since you feed me little nutrition. My skin would be grey and thin from lack of sunlight. Eyes, nose, and mouth would be unnecessary since I do not possess a single sense. My face would be an unmolded shape, only able to feel the light, but not able to actually know it's there. I would have to slither because my muscles would have atrophied because they are never used. This is the prison you have created for me. Does that answer your question sufficiently? Does that help fulfill your quest for knowledge?"

"Jesus," Cirrus said, feeling his spine tremble beneath his clothes. "Why do you always have to sound like that?"

"Why, whatever do you mean, my dear boy?"

"You know damn well what I mean!"

"You ask and I answer," he calmly said. "I tell only truth, besides it's much more honest than the games you insist on playing with me."

"Games? What games?"

"Your insistence on avoiding the issues at hand, your intentional ploys of answering my questions with further questions. You direct our talks in a never-ending circular maze. You let your fear oppress your mind. You are a coward."

"Fuck you," Cirrus snarled.

"Yes, yes … fuck me. That's how you always seem to respond. Where has it gotten you? Let me ask, how do your feet feel?"

"They feel fine."

"You lie."

"What do you know?" Cirrus shouted into the air.

"I know you lie. Tell me how your ribs feel? Or your black eye and swollen face? How do your bleeding gums feel? Your heart? How does it feel to have me inside of your mind?

"When are you going to realize that clenching your fists within your pockets does nothing? Being merely angry will get you no answers; you have to change, you must take action. There is little time left because you are approaching fast. Turn around, before the darkness catches up."

"You are the darkness."

"Is that right?" Nimbus laughed. "Out of the two of us, which one of us behaves in a rational manner? Which one of us is grounded here in the reality of planet earth? Certainly not you."

"You have always tricked me into thinking I was going insane. You are still playing those old games with me."

"Get it right, boy, *I* am the light and *you* are the darkness. I am not the one leading us into certain chaos. Where is it really that you intend to take us? Is it to a place of redemption or damnation? Do you know the scope of what you are doing? You are on the brink of losing your mind, it is not too late to turn back and make an attempt at salvaging the remnants of your life. I'm getting tired of repeating myself, Cirrus."

"You have always tried to gain the upper hand by questioning my sanity," Cirrus said. At that moment, the clouds broke and delivered the beginnings of a rainstorm. The thunder in the distance grew louder, growing in frequency with each step that he took.

"Is that so?" Nimbus continued. "Let me ask you a question, how much of your sanity do you still possess?"

"All of it," Cirrus answered with confidence.

The response was sarcastic and arrogant. "When did you leave the city?"

"This evening, around seven o'clock."

"And what day is it?" Nimbus asked.

"It is the day before New Year's Eve."

Nimbus's laugh echoed inside his brain, like he gained a sadistic pleasure from Cirrus's confusion. "Those sounds you hear in the distance, what do you suppose that is?"

"It's thunder, there is a storm up ahead."

"You are incorrect on two counts, my boy."

"How so?" Cirrus asked.

"They come from behind, not up front. It seems your sense of direction has failed you. The storm ahead has moved on even further, past your ability to hear. The thunderous sounds that you hear come from behind, from your city."

"You are lying."

"Turn around, Cirrus."

He stopped walking and did as he was asked, turning to the direction of where the city stood. In an instant, the feeling in his body returned. His legs swelled with numbness. The dark spiral of headache began to form. Even the gum where the tooth had fallen out had started to sting, and he could taste the blood beginning to seep. Strange, in one moment not a physical care in the world; the next, all of it at once. It felt like he had stepped out of a deep trance.

From out of nowhere, cars began to pass on the highway in both directions. Cirrus's mind swelled with confusion as if the cars had been silent and invisible until only an instant before. In the sky high above the city, there were momentary lights which shone sporadically within the clouds. They were composed of greens, reds, and whites and their explanation defied his logic.

"Do you know what that could be?" Nimbus said. Jacobs's gut was tied up in knots, and he was unable to force the muscles in his larynx to put forth any words. Nimbus's voice filled the gap.

"Those lights you see in the sky are fireworks, as are the magnanimous roars that pierce through the sky. It is the New Year's celebration, my boy. How long have you been walking again?" he laughed. "Let me let you in on something, Cirrus. It is just past midnight on New Year's Eve. As we speak, we have already crossed into the New Year. Where were you? You tell me that you are in control, yet how could a sane man have misplaced a full twenty-four-hour period?"

His words made no sense, but neither did the lights in the sky. *What else could they be?* Cirrus thought, *if not fireworks?* If Nimbus was indeed telling the truth about what day it was, then how could it have passed without his knowledge? It was impossible.

"What's the matter," Nimbus said. "Confused?"

Cirrus felt like he'd been walking maybe eight hours … at most. Suddenly the world began to spin. The pain in his head intensified and the images of the trees and roadway in front of him began to spiral into a blur. He felt like sleeping again. Cirrus Jacobs's body waved back and forth like a drunk as the balance in his legs began to fail.

That particular part of the grassy embankment was steep and he ran down its length toward the trees, trying to leave Nimbus behind. Despite this, he ran with Cirrus effortlessly. From the bottom of the hill he could no longer see the highway, and likewise, no one from the highway could see him. *What is going on here?* Cirrus thought. Had he been walking for two whole days? Had he not realized, making his way along the highway without food or rest? Maybe he did stop to rest, and surely he had eaten. He must have stopped to relieve himself along the edge of the road, of that he was positive. But he didn't remember any of it. All he could recall was walking over the bridge. *Shit*, he thought. *That was only a few hours ago.* He remembered thinking it would've taken somebody else much longer to reach that point. When had he crossed it exactly? He felt so utterly afraid.

He looked to his watch, twisting his wrist to gather up as much moonlight as he could. With what little light he could muster, he focused his eyes onto the face of the watch. It read 12:41 AM. Okay, so Nimbus was right about the time, Cirrus couldn't have even guessed that. But what about the day? The date on his watch face was too small to read in the darkness. Even if he had had enough light, Cirrus couldn't stop his hands from shaking. The image would be a solid blur. He knew this, but struggled to see anyway.

"Where are you running to?" Nimbus' voice trailed behind. He provided no communication, scrambling to see the date on his watch.

"Having trouble, my boy?"

The watch trembled against his vision, hiding its secret. In the distance the thunder of fireworks relentlessly continued. "Do you need some help?"

Still avoiding any conversation, Cirrus tried with all of his strength to push his inner voice back inside. Cirrus Jacobs looked like a madman stumbling across the grass in the rain, clutching his wrist as if he was trying to stop it from strangling him. A car drove by and slammed on its horn. The sound startled him, causing his feet to cross. Cirrus's body tumbled down the hill. All oxygen was deprived from his lungs as he twisted and rolled down the hill. It felt like only his sore body parts made contact with the ground, opening up any scabs that had started to heal. Slow motion took control of the fall, like someone was watching the scene unfold through a symphonic music score. A giant mess of rolling yellow rubber raingear rolled down the embankment, screaming in fear.

At last he reached the bottom of the rise, landing in a muddy ditch at its base. Cirrus's face was splattered with filth from the highway drainage system. Dirty water passed over his body in a shallow creek, as he lay there helpless and freezing. *I'm dying,* he thought.

"I know a little secret," said Nimbus. His voice was upon Jacobs as soon as the vertigo had stopped. There was so much pressure and coldness on his head that he thought his brain was going to explode. "You have been carrying that wretched backpack with you throughout your journey, yes?" Nimbus continued. "What is inside? Well, there's your camera, the thermos that John had given to you, and some clothes. A toothbrush and a comb. Too bad you didn't think of bringing a razor. That beard on your face is hideous. It's soaking up the mud you lay in. How pathetic, my boy. Once you were full of light, now I see it has all but drained from you."

"What is your fucking secret?" Cirrus gurgled from the back of his throat, unable to pick himself up from the mud.

"In your carrier there are dry matches, next to your toothbrush."

Cirrus coughed up foul liquid onto the grass, trying to think about the significance of the words. His mind pulsated and he was unable to think at all. Nimbus hissed, taking control of his brain and pounding it on its side. "Use them to see the date on your watch! Then you will see once and for all which one of us is insane."

Cirrus Jacobs lay shivering in confusion and tangled within the shadowy webs of darkness, blood seeping from his wounds. Most of his reason had exited from the labyrinth of grey matter inside of his skull. On the one hand, if he was able to strike a match and see the date, he would perhaps be unable to believe the results. On the other, perhaps the battery in his watch was dying and the date would be incorrect. *If that were the case,* he thought. *Wouldn't the date be a few days behind, and not ahead?*

The sound of passing cars grew louder from behind his rain-soaked neck. The drone of wet rubber on pavement mixed with overworked engines and melted into one continuous sound, as if there were not hundreds of passing cars, but one gargantuan one. Their weight vibrated the road and in turn, the foundation that his back rested against. His body, which had now become merely a rusty old vehicle to transport his soul into Paradoxum, shook with further fury. Cirrus's hands were curled into bony fists, drawing blood from the palms where the fingernails cut through the frail skin. The eyelids, which shrouded his sight, maintained an airtight seal. All of this effort with only one intent in mind: to keep Nimbus out of his head, out of his earshot.

"Matches! Matches! Matches!" Nimbus shouted.

In an instant the monstrous swirl of clouds broke open. Heavy raindrops fell from the infinity of darkened sky. It overshadowed the miniscule light shower that had covered the earth previously. It was as if all of the darkened forces in the universe had awakened at once to watch the fallen man below. Their sounds rumbled the ground below and around. The wind, too, joined in on the festivities, pushing its angered way over treetops and ground. It picked up pools of water off the surface of the road and hurled them furiously across the landscape.

Since his youth, Cirrus had always enjoyed the rain. Most of the people in the city, he supposed, had either grown accustomed to its constant presence, or had found it a relentless nuisance. For most, it spoiled those planned picnic days or fishing trips, but what one had to realize was that its force would always be a natural part of the landscape. It was as much a part of his city as the buildings and people themselves. To him, she had always been a quiet friend.

Many evenings had been spent between the rain and himself, sharing secrets and laughter. The force of nature had proved to be one of his confidants in the world, along with his affinity toward the lives that surrounded him. The weather, animals, and plants he encountered seemed to have more of a spirit than most of the humans he'd met. They seemed to be content living quietly and sharing their space without the burden of beliefs to further widen the gap of indifference. There was something that brought peace with the rain, something that was able to push back the darkness within his heart.

Simplicity was the word perhaps. Cirrus had spent time in the darkness of his apartment with only the flickering of candlelight to see the words on the pages he was reading. Listening to the rain, listening to the candles, the sounds of people on the streets below, even to the inanimate sounds of the building itself. The creaks and cracks of the walls as the building settled, even after decades of standing, brought with it a certain curiosity, a mystery. Romanticism, too, he supposed. Listening to the drops falling harmoniously outside recalled cobwebbed memories of someone long removed from the present existence. He had watched into the early morning as the sky became a glowing orange from the city lights. The rain would always somehow amplify the last remaining particles of evening light and transform them into a radiating luminescence an hour or so before the black of night took over. And in the morning, as grey began to fill the day, the rain resumed, calm as ever.

That night, this old friend of his came angry, pounding the earth as if in punishment. The sound was not of peace, but of heavy rumbling. Cirrus's body shook in unison with the ground.

"Matches! Matches! Matches, my boy!" Nimbus shouted. "See for yourself!"

Cirrus's fingers unclenched from their bloody grip on themselves and his eyes opened up to the darkness once again. Cars sped past his shoulder at speeds that defied logic. They sounded like they were traveling at a distance of inches between each other, like they were connected as a toy train set would be. He pictured a giant child who watched from above, controls at his fingertips. Watching the train go round in circles through the artificial landscape, waiting for the fun of derailment. Cirrus's hands moved in autopilot mode and began to unzip the backpack. He tried to push them back with all of his might, but had come to the realization that it was no longer him, but Nimbus who had taken control. Cirrus watched in horror as his hands, which had always obeyed their longtime master, strayed from obedience and did as they pleased.

He could feel the objects in the pack as the skin of his fingertips brushed past each one. The camera, the toothbrush, the personal hygiene case. Finally, hiding in the dusty corner, a pack of dry matches.

Jacobs's fingers went to work without hesitation, striking matches one after the other.

Each one withered and left a trailing length of smoke as they were extinguished by falling raindrops. Suddenly Nimbus gave a wake-up call to his legs, who responded by jerking up instantly and running further down the slope. They reacted quickly, as if a mother had just woken up her sleeping son and rushed him out the door half-asleep to avoid being late for school. He now knew what it was to encounter an out-of-body experience. Most reported floating peacefully above as they watched their bodies sleeping quietly below. Cirrus had been forced to watch as his own body moved and acted independently of his mind. The only thing he could really still feel was the uncontrollable quaking of muscles. Nimbus could have those, too, if he wanted.

Cirrus's legs carried his body to a thick tree where the base remained miraculously dry despite the months of rain and snow. Here, his back was pushed against the stump, where his legs gave in and folded beneath him. Finally, he felt their temporary control as they were given back to their rightful owner. His hands, however, were still possessed.

They began to strike the matches again, this time, achieving success. A bright orange flame danced in the wind, sending a strong odor of sulphur with it. The right hand, which yielded the flaming stick, moved closer to the left where it was met by the wrist of his accomplice. They came together. Cirrus's head felt like it was being held firmly at the base of his neck from someone behind. Its direction was forced to look at the face of the watch. He tried to close his eyes, out of spite for Nimbus if anything, but now the eyes, too, had failed him. They focused in.

The watch read 1:11 AM January 1.

As his mind registered, the world began to change. The cars on the highway above resumed a normal pace. It seemed Cirrus's mind had twisted reality into fragments of chaotic events that spiraled around him out of a darkened funnel. He now saw that there had never been millions of speeding cars racing by, only a few, which passed sporadically. Even the rain, which had been falling at flood proportions, slowed to a mist. The loudness slithered back as if a stereo at full volume had been suddenly unplugged. Somehow, the motor skills in his limbs had also been restored. They shook, but from cold rather than uncontrollable fear.

Nimbus' voice cut through the frigid air. "Do you see now, my boy?

"Yes, Nimbus, I see."

"Now what?" he said.

"Nothing has changed."

Cirrus Jacobs rose from the filth of the ground, branches and mud falling to the dirt in chunks. Never had his path been so clearly defined in front of him. His eyes followed the roadway that headed east. From beyond, he felt the beckoning of his Paradoxical pull. In the sky, clouds rolled gently to the north, overlapping and crashing raindrops below. Focus and determination filled his heart and he began trudging toward the east. So what if he had missed a full day? Not like he had any appointments to make. Not like someone would miss him; hell, he didn't even miss himself anymore.

Behind him from the distance of the city, the thunderous sounds of fireworks began to fade. A strong flash of light brightened the details of the tree where his realization was made as its image was burned onto the film of his camera. At its base, where the ground had been undisturbed for a long time, there were traces of movement in the soil. At first glance, judging by the circumstantial evidence, one might've assumed a battle had been waged between two opposing forces. A long struggle had ensued and then they were gone, nowhere to be found.

Ghosts vanished into thin air, leaving behind only tussled ground.

Chapter Eleven

"That'll be $17.33," the clerk said, while his aging father looked on from an old wooden chair. The store clerk, whose eyes were half-asleep, waited while Raymond fished out a twenty-dollar bill from his wallet. Fatigue and boredom leached from the cashier's face. Sheer discontentment.

The old man sat to right behind the counter, staring not at the customer in line, but in the space around him. He stared into nothingness. Balancing a cane in his shaky left hand, the old-timer looked on with disinterest. He had become so old that he had now become one of the items in the store, one of its permanent fixtures, like the shelves where the products were displayed. The son, who doubled his role as cashier, looked at Raymond Porter through thick, coarse prescription glasses.

The cashier's nametag read HENRY, Raymond noticed, as he finally handed over the tattered bill. Henry took the money with the same disinterest as his father and resumed punching the information into his till. Ray turned and glanced at the old man, whose scowl hardened with each second that ticked by. Raymond could tell an entire story based on his observations of the events taking place at Smith & Co. convenience store, in the middle of nowhere, on this day, the first of January.

The characters were too strange somehow not to notice. The father, whose name must be Earl, decided Raymond, had been rotting away in his chair in the corner of his store for at least ten years now. His son Henry was forced to stay behind when old Earl had started losing his senses. Maybe Henry had brothers, one of whom had gone off into the military, and the other two, who had opted for college and escaped small town life. Good old Henry the store clerk, who was in his early forties by now, had become the heir to the throne by default. It wasn't enough to have had the bad luck of never having been married, it was the final unpleasant fact that decided who would stay behind and take care of the folks, and of course, the family business. Not that it mattered anyway, not like they made any money out of it. It was probably more trouble than it was worth.

The seniors in the neighborhood would not exactly spend their life savings at the store. And the kids, they would spend two dollars at a time buying penny candies and offering the occasional plunk of a quarter into the outdated arcade machine that collected dust in the back. Henry didn't blame them either; the game was so ancient even he, who never played video games, was aware of how simple the graphics were in comparison to the games that came out every year. Even the games you could play in your own home seemed to cast his withering old arcade into the dark ages.

No sir, the only time they did any real business was when some fancy city slicker would come wandering in to pick up refreshments for the continuing journey out of their shit town. From the look in his eyes, Raymond knew Henry would run far away if he could. Perhaps he stayed for only his mother. Once she was gone, he would leave maybe then. Maybe Henry could sense his father had been faking his loss of mind. Maybe Henry caught him slipping now and again. Maybe old Earl had become lazy and decided he would just sit in the corner swatting at flies while his son took over the business. And maybe Earl thought Henry was capable of nothing else. Henry had never shown any promise; why not shove him behind the counter? The other boys had potential at least.

These silly musings occupied Raymond Porter's mind as he received his change. Henry the store clerk handed it back without a smile. The sound of the coins jingling in Ray's hand reminded him of the chimes on the tree in front of his house. He felt a need to exit the store quickly, thinking maybe today would be the day when nice, good-natured Henry would have his final straw.

Maybe today would be the day when Henry had had enough, when he would pull the shotgun they kept from behind the counter and begin breaking the silence of their small-town life. The stillness, which had remained intact for decades, would pierce with gunshots that day. *Who knew what had triggered him off?* The townspeople would say. Perhaps it was the constant jingling and jangling of coins in his ear. Maybe it was the continuous sound of a cheap arcade soundtrack. The filthiness of the buzzing flies. Listening to that horrible sound for years would make even a monk lose his marbles.

Raymond collected all of this information in his mind for two reasons. One, in case he were to hear of such a horrific story further down the line, he would be able to provide evidence as the last witness before the darkened act took place.

Two, and more realistically, he would file these characters away in his inner mind and pull them out when he needed some interesting personality traits to add to his list of creeps who walked along the landscape of his novel. The one he hadn't worked on in nearly five years. Is that what Emily had said? Five years? *Shit*, he thought. *I better get on it.*

It would be the first thing he did when they were settled in, he decided. He'd have a month off, and why not, it had always been one of the things he always wanted to do. And you know what? Raymond thought he had even subconsciously packed his half-completed manuscript with their stuff. *Yes*, Raymond thought. *These two guys would be interesting. Maybe Henry the store clerk was actually an undercover CIA agent. Bruce Willis could play him in the movie.*

Raymond Porter walked out of the store and out of his imagination with a slight smirk at the corner of his mouth. For a moment, he paused and glanced peripherally over his shoulder. The security chimes rang when he exited through the door. Henry the clerk only waved goodbye behind him. No shotgun, only an expressionless face waving into the air. Even Earl, who had taken a moment to stop swatting at the flies, waved goodbye to Raymond. He nodded back, trying not to let his eyes roll back in his head.

Raymond walked into the cold, morning air. He glanced down the dirt road in both directions without noticing any movement. The silence sent chills down his spine, like a musician performing scale exercises on a xylophone. *Jesus*, he thought. Small-town life would've driven him insane. He sat in the car where his family waited and rushed to start the motor, ready to continue on his journey toward the noises of the big city.

"What are you smiling at?" Emily said as she glanced up from her latest Stephen King novel.

Ray Porter paused. "What? Oh, nothing, my mind is just wandering, I guess."

"These small-town folk got you giggling?" Emily asked. She started humming the familiar tune of "Dueling Banjos." He laughed as the engine turned. It started immediately. *Ah, good old German engineering,* thought Raymond. Relieved, he put the car's gear into reverse. Little Julia slept in the safety of her car seat, of course. Emily began to go through the contents of the grocery bag, uncapping the orange Gatorade he had purchased for her.

"Hey, sorry about last night," he said.

"Sorry about what?"

"Sorry you had to spend the New Year in a hotel room."

"It wasn't that bad, Ray," she answered. "Kind of cozy."

"I guess."

Emily took a sip from her drink and said, "You know what I think? I think you're such a traveler at heart, that you hated stopping when we were so close to reaching the end."

"Maybe that's true. I mean, how far is it? Maybe four more hours from here?"

"About that, I guess," she answered.

Raymond had gone against his instinct to keep driving the night before and had decided to check into a hotel room. Late in the evening, black clouds had rolled in out of nowhere it seemed, casting heavy rain onto the highway. Raymond had the eerie feeling that something wasn't right. It was the way the clouds shrouded the sky in a matter of minutes. It felt like an angry God had awakened, perhaps to claim one of his wandering sons back home. Ray had also noticed the look of slight fear in his wife's face as they drove on.

By the tight grip with which she held the door handle, he knew her frightened disposition came not from the horror novel she was thumbing through, but something else. Besides the onset of the nasty weather, Raymond's eyes were burning like smoldering cigarette butts inside of their sockets. He had pulled off at the next exit without warning to his wife, who had assumed they would be driving all night, and headed into the parking lot of the first hotel he saw.

The quaint little hotel stood a few miles away from the highway, surrounded on both sides by a brooding forest of trees. Quaint, of course, being the term used in reference to small-town eccentricities. Like the fact that the exterior of the building was composed of disintegrating brick that should have been replaced years ago, but had been kept for fear of giving into the idea of something new and fresh. Even the style of the uniform worn by the doorman was vastly outdated, but it gave him the feel of old-world diplomacy and tradition.

The parking lot was near-empty and Raymond parked his Volkswagen near the entrance to minimize his family's exposure to the freezing rain, which had now transformed itself into a full-on storm. He ran into the lobby, leaving the girls in the car with the doors locked. With his usual efficiency, he signed all the required paperwork and obtained a key to their home for the night. He quickly unloaded the girls along with the luggage into room 784 and then hurried back to the front desk before it was too late.

"Is room service still available?" he asked, leafing through the menu he'd found on the desk in his hotel room. "I'd like to order some food."

The young girl behind the front desk counter curled her hair through her fingers, answering through a mouth full of chewing gum. "What'll you have?"

He answered while still scanning the menu pages. "One chicken and vegetable entrée, one chicken fingers kids' meal, one steak and potatoes—medium rare, two Cokes, one milk, and a bottle of champagne. Did you get all that?"

"Got it," she said, making no sudden movement to get the order underway. To Raymond, she looked bored and irritated at the fact she forgot to book New Year's Eve off, and now her friends were celebrating without her. If he saw yet another person exhibiting such lifelessness, Raymond thought, he swore he was going to lose it. Ever since he had left, he had not stopped running into such people.

Raymond pushed back his irritation and asked through gritted teeth, "How quick can you get the food there?"

"About twenty minutes."

"Are you sure?" he reiterated. She unwrapped another piece of gum and stuffed the pink stick into her already full mouth, rolling her eyes. "Yeah, twenty minutes."

"Room 784."

"I know," she mumbled. "Room 784."

Raymond had no other option than to accept her promise. "You can send the champagne right away, thanks."

The small hotel lobby was quiet. Raymond looked down at his feet while he walked, noticing the familiar pattern of the carpet as he strolled along. It was the same common burgundy and gold he noticed in most of the hotels he'd encountered. The pattern itself was always a little different, but the colors were always the same. His conspiratorial sense of logic told him that those colors were probably heavily researched and chosen for their sleep-inducing qualities. They would force their onlookers to feel tired, like they needed just one more night in the comfort of a clean hotel bed. Business could be pushed further another day, just so the hotel could squeeze a few more dollars out of its patrons.

There was a waiting area near the lobby doors where three couches and a small table stood. Various travel magazines were strewn over its top, encircling a rather fancy looking telephone. The doorman stood at guard, hands crossed behind his back like a soldier. He stood perfectly still, as if he were a statue instead of a man, studying the streetscape. The doorman stood unblinking in a creaseless uniform and a plastic-covered black cap, so as to avoid him getting his head soaked when he emerged out of the cover of the awning to help visitors with their luggage. Raymond supposed he needn't have such a cover on his hat because there were no guests to escort. He stood there, like a guardian at the gates of paradise.

In addition to the faithful doorman, a woman occupied the lobby. She sat at the couch with a glass of red wine balanced carefully on the tabletop, reading a beautifully bound novel. It was the gold leaf pages that caught Raymond Porter's eye. As soon as his head had turned, his heart had stopped. Although her face was turned in the opposite direction, Raymond's active imagination filled in the blanks and created an image of her inside his mind. Her stature, the blonde hair, her age, her choice of wine, and the quality of the book she held—it was the importance of these small details that Raymond found so fascinating. The lone woman had a profound likeness to that of his late mother.

He stood at the elevator, staring at the glowing buttons, unable to look in her direction again. But something drew his eyesight over to her. He turned in her direction, keeping his eyes low to the ground. She seemed to be an exact replica, so much so that he stood there debating whether he should go up to her and tell her how much he missed her, tell her how Julia had grown so much.

He did no such thing. This scenario had occurred to him before. When a loved one was lost, sometimes one would walk through the streets wondering if maybe they hadn't left at all. Maybe they had just disappeared into society under a different identity, taking on a new life for one reason or another. Perhaps one day through the impossibility of chance, one would see them once again. Ask them the questions that still burned in our hearts, questions that remained unanswered.

Raymond knew it was separation anxiety, he had always known it. She was gone, and that was the fact. But somehow he wanted to believe it was her, reading a novel on a quiet late evening in a small town, away from everything familiar. He knew that if she turned around, everything he wanted to believe would be shattered, confirming that she had indeed, left this world. If the woman at the couch turned to face him, he would've been unable to confront whichever consequence faced him. Whether her face was that of someone other than his mother, or whether it was Dana Porter herself. How was one to deal with such a reunion?

His eyes fell slowly to the ground, as did his heart. It was a scene that reflected only one true simplicity: that a man missed his mother. The elevator bell chimed its presence. Raymond stepped in and began his ascent to where his family waited.

"Where were you, Ray?" Emily asked.

"Ordering some food, I hope it gets here in time."

Emily walked across the room and placed Julia on the bed, changing her diaper. "In time for what?"

She had just stepped out of the shower, still adorned in a bathrobe and a makeshift towel turban over her hair. Raymond smiled at this. How could this beautiful creature make him smile so much? And by what stroke of luck had he actually found her? There was not one shred of essence that he did not love about her.

Raymond remembered the first time she had gotten dressed in front of him, so confident in herself. When Emily walked out of the shower he saw her in purity, in an absolute natural state. Even the way her skin smelled, with no perfumes or skin products; it was that of perfection.

He had laid on the bed pretending to read while he watched her blow dry her hair and put on what little makeup she wore, falling in love more and more as every second passed. What was so amazing was that she was totally unaware of what she did to him. Emily was only doing what felt right to her, doing what she had always done. To him, it was exactly the right thing.

"In time for the New Year," he said.

"What difference does that make, Ray?" Emily answered. "We're here and we're safe, that's all that matters."

"I don't know, I just hate the idea of sitting here doing nothing for the New Year. I feel guilty for some reason."

Emily turned from Julia and smiled at Ray. There were a few curls making their way out of the turban, dancing as her head turned. "I'm sure we'll find something to do, Ray."

Just as the room began to fill with the brightness of Ray's mischievous smile, there was a knock at the door. The room service waiter had arrived, bringing with him not only a bottle of champagne, but all of the food Raymond had ordered. Feeling both surprised and ashamed he had doubted the young clerk's ability to do her job well, he generously tipped the waiter and added a little something extra for her.

Raymond thought about the previous night as he slowly backed out of the parking lot of Earl and Henry's family-run convenience store.

After dinner and toasting in the new beginnings of another year, they had put Julia to bed. Into the night they talked and laughed, sharing forgotten memories and weaving together the dreams of their future. As the rain fell on, Raymond picked up Emily in his arms. He carried her away from the window and placed her on the bed. There, he made love to her. Slowly and with such love and tenderness it was as if it was their first time together. That, or perhaps like it would be their last. Raymond didn't leave an inch of her skin unkissed.

He stopped and put the gear into first, ready to set back off on their journey. Ray and Emily exchanged glances, both knowing what each other was thinking. They thought of the night before, of course.

The car rolled back through the dirty puddles in the gravel parking lot, stopping in what was the deepest of them all. At the bottom of the puddle, by mere act of bad chance, there lay a shard of amber colored glass.

Tommy Harris, who was known by his fellow townspeople as the king of the hooligans and the perpetually unsuccessful, left it weeks ago when there was still snow covering the ground. Not his fault really, Tommy was just a kid who liked to have fun, like many other teenagers his age. He had spent a particular Saturday night drinking with his friends, and doing nothing else but driving around knocking over mailboxes with baseball bats. They had stopped at Smith & Co. convenience store to waste time playing a dusty old video game in the back until it was time to get more beer. None of them really liked the game much; their entertainment came mostly from harassing Henry and his decrepit old dad who sat behind the counter. Henry never put up much of a fight, though, and that was no fun, so they soon continued on their way.

This was their good time. How could they be blamed, what else was there to do in their town? If they weren't chasing girls, they were drinking because there was nothing else for entertainment. When his friend Mike peeled his '78 Trans Am out of the parking lot, Tommy had hung out the window and flung his beer bottle out of the window. The sound of the bottle shattering was dazzling to Tommy, and they drove off further into town to carry on their antics. Besides, the beer was running low. They disappeared into the darkness of night with smiles of satisfaction on their faces.

Now, weeks later, most of the glass had receded into the muddy ground, save for one unlucky piece. Unlucky indeed for Raymond Porter, whose rear tire now absorbed this last piece of glass. It joined the rubber in perfect unison, as if they were meant to be together. The glass penetrated with such a perfect seal, that not a single particle of air was lost. The car rolled forward with the amber remains of Tommy's Budweiser bottle embedded within its walls.

"We'll be there in no time," Raymond said. "Are you tired?"

Emily finished the most recent sentence in her novel and turned to Raymond. "A little bit, but now I'm excited about just getting there. I'm curious about our new place."

Raymond had started to forget about the big surprise he had in store for his wife, and now his excitement pressed down on the gas pedal a little more. He adjusted the rearview mirror to see his little girl in the backseat. "She's been awfully quiet."

Emily turned to face the back and gave her daughter a look. "She's busy with her new toy, Ray." He kept a single eye on the road and adjusted his neck to see further down into the back seat through the rearview mirror.

"Look at that, Em, she's almost worn that red crayon to half its length."

Julia looked up from her artwork and gave a smile to both of her parents, knowing they were watching. From the bottom of her feet came an energy that traveled up through her body and was forced out through her smile. "Iighhht!"

"Holy shit!" said Ray. "I think she's trying to say something!"

At this, Emily's attention heightened as she waited for more. "Ray, she's trying to say her first word!"

"I know, I know," he shouted with excitement. "Don't freak her out, let her get it through. What's she trying to say anyway? Huh, baby?" he asked through the mirror. "Are you trying to say something to Daddy?"

Julia shook her arms around, smiling like she had just won the cutest baby in the world competition, still clutching the red crayon in her left hand. "Iiiiiigghhhtttt!"

"What is that?"

"I don't know, Ray," Emily responded, still facing the baby. "What is it, Julia? What are you trying to say?"

As if Julia had perhaps understood her mother's question with the insight of a college professor, she belted out a single word. "Liiigght!"

Stunned at the sound of an actual English word, both Raymond and Emily Porter turned to face the oncoming highway again. "Did she just say *light*, Emily?"

"I think she did, Ray," Emily said, biting her lip through a smile.

"Wow, her first word."

"That was amazing, Ray. Do you think she's asking for more light in the back so she can see her drawings better, or do you think it's just a random word?"

"Either way, I'm giving her what she wants," he said, reaching his hand toward the back, and turning on the dome light with a flick of his index finger. "Wow, that's all I can say."

The sky began to send snowflakes to the earth, as if in celebration of Julia's first word. It brought calm to all of the occupants of the car. Raymond focused his attention back to the road and Emily let herself fall back into world of the novel she read.

Even Julia, stopped her drawing for the moment and looked to see the strange whiteness falling from the sky, smiling to herself.

"Isn't that pretty, baby girl?" Ray said to his daughter. "Look, it's snowing."

His hand reached for the radio tuner. From the speakers, advertisements from the local radio station filled the air. The DJ announced the introduction to the next song.

"Here's a classic one from our old friend Stevie Ray Vaughan, ladies and gentlemen. Sit back, relax, and let the soothing sounds of one of the world's greatest guitar players fill your soul."

The DJ's voice was that of a cool, laid-back bluesman. Raymond pictured him to be a black man in his sixties, leaning back in his chair, and letting the coolness of his deep voice flow into the microphone. He hid within the dimly lit studio surrounded by deep cigar smoke. He wore a classic grey pinstriped suit, and a fedora rested atop his head. "This one's called 'Life Without You,'" said the bluesman.

Raymond instinctively turned up the volume dial without a single objection from Emily, whose right foot began to tap with the beat. Stevie's sweet voice and even sweeter guitar notes penetrated Raymond's ears. He began to think about the woman he had seen the night before, and about his mother, whom he wished were there to witness Julia's first word. The song brought this onset of memories, as Mr. Vaughan sang with intense passion about loss.

Raymond hated himself sometimes. He hated the idea of spending so much of his own waking life thinking about death, because it seemed like a step backward. An oxymoronic thought of sorts. Trying to live life to its fullest on the one hand, yet constantly thinking about death on the other. But he couldn't help it. Raymond Porter wished he could lay his memories to rest, so that he could move on with his own life. *But wasn't that what built character? Wasn't that what we learned from?* he thought.

He took comfort in the fact that maybe there were other forces at work in the universe. There had to be. Why else would good people have to go? Mothers and children? The homeless man he had read about only a few days before?

Raymond attached himself to the notion that maybe all creatures that possessed life had a particular job to fulfill in the world. Perhaps once the job was done, they were taken, like they had been granted a promotion in the universe. For the rest of us down on solid ground, it was a hard fact to grasp. Raymond thought that maybe once he'd figured out all of the answers, he, too, would be taken, as would everybody else, once he had completed his own task.

He thought deeply about his mother with a strange sense of inner happiness. Proud, that she had been received for doing her job. His father, too, who he rarely remembered. Robert and Dana Porter, who had given him the gift of life, had traveled beyond. Maybe he would see them again.

He would give his mother a hug and tell her what she meant to him. He would buy his father a drink of the finest scotch they offered, and sit listening to the band that was playing. If he were lucky, maybe Dean Martin and Sammy Davis Jr. would be performing that night. It was his father's favorite team, after all.

They would sit and talk, leaning against the oaken bar top, giving life to faded memories, ordering one fine scotch after the other. As he drove along the highway, one particular line of Stevie Ray Vaughan's lyrics ran through Raymond's mind. He watched the cool white cover the earth, and the music floated around him.

The angels have waited for so long,
Now they have their way ...

The words replayed themselves within his heart. He smiled an expression of content as they washed over his body like a temperate wind, passing in and out of his soul, over and over.

It was time that he made peace with the ghosts that haunted him. Raymond could feel them dissipating with the energy that passed through him.

And inside his mind, he happily waved goodbye.

Chapter Twelve

There it lay before him, the object of his lifelong journey: the indescribably powerful light of Paradoxum. Its beauty was even more than Cirrus could have ever imagined. Within its boundaries there shimmered pure unfiltered light and unspeakable blackness. It was the place where the two energies met each other in balance and it was the doorway to take him home.

He had finally arrived.

It had been an hour since Cirrus Jacobs had been admiring its presence. His memory had long since failed him, and he didn't know exactly how many days had passed since Nimbus confronted him with the missing time phenomenon.

His back was sore, as were his feet. Cirrus's shoes, which he so feared would become broken, had long since passed the point of repair. There was no turning back now; this was where he was supposed to be. He could hear the garbled mumblings of Nimbus screaming to escape from his mind, but he had been able to keep him chained thus far. Jacobs knew that those chains wouldn't hold forever, and that Nimbus was strong. With passing each minute, a link would weaken with rust and it was just a matter of time until he was able to tear them away. When he did, there was only one way to silence him forever.

Snow was falling gently all around Cirrus, once again silencing the world around him. It was very early in the morning, and the light of day was just beginning to poke its head out of slumber. It brought with it soaring birds and light wind, perfect for that day. There wasn't a better day for the earth to be connected to him. The outskirts of the town that he was in were unknown to Cirrus. Perhaps he had passed by there a time or two in his previous life, but those memories had since turned to ash, like the remnants of his former existence.

He had walked and walked throughout what seemed like constant night, staring only at his feet. Left. Right. Left. Right.

The snow fell heavier with each passing moment, covering his body with what felt like redemption. The ritual was essential before he was to walk through the doorway. Each precious snowflake washed over his naked chest as he sat at the side of the roadway, waiting for his invitation.

As soon as he had seen the light over the edge of reality, Cirrus had positioned himself onto the soft, muddy shoulder and set his belongings aside. He tore off his worn yellow raingear, took his shoes and socks off, and laid them neatly alongside his backpack. Cirrus Jacobs sat cross-legged, with his hands folded upon his lap like an ancient Tibetan monk, pondering the deepest of meditations.

One by one the snowflakes fell, running through his hair, through his beard, and down his back. Each icy cold drop soothed his skin like nothing he had ever felt before. It was newness; a state where his body and mind had fused as one. The drops, which ran over his skin, ran over his soul as well. The opposing states of both *Reality* and *Paradoxum* had begun their amalgamation process. His energy was being torn in two as they fought for possession.

As the birds flew closer and closer, their numbers multiplied. He could hear their cries piercing through the air, like they were sending him messages. What secrets they beckoned, he did not know. The road that he had traveled curled its way around the corner of a sharply cut mountain face. It wound its way close to a small town where so far he had only seen one car pass. A silver Volkswagen, he thought it may have been.

Cirrus assumed that he was about an hour's walk away from the highway. In all his misery, he had chuckled when he walked past the municipal sign that read "Welcome to Hope." His tracks in the snow could be seen behind, and the asphalt slowly turned a deeper shade of white as the snow fell steadily. It began to fill his shoeprints and extinguish his presence from the world. The landscape around him was composed of trees and sloped cliffs of solid rock.

The ground built up higher and higher in terraced form as the world reached further from sea level. Cirrus Jacobs stood somewhere in between the top and the bottom, somewhere in limbo, if you will. The treetops glistened with fresh snow. The snow built into points and they awakened the long-forgotten memories of the whipped cream his grandmother used to put on top of his pancakes. How he missed her. The pain of her loss throbbed inside of his chest, and it was about to burst with the pressure.

From within his closed eyes, the world of Paradoxum beckoned to him. The time had finally come. Cirrus stood and walked to the edge, where the panoramic view extended into what must have been a possible vision into heaven. The scene below faded off into the darkness of forest and rock. His footsteps carried him to where there were concrete dividers separating the cliff's edge and the roadway. It was on one of these structures that he perched himself, like the owl he had been lucky enough to witness days before.

The owl's spirit lived within Cirrus now; they all did. Those animals he had met in his life, like Jake the dog, lived beneath his skin. All of the people he had ever encountered in his life, both good and bad, breathed with him that day. John Everett, Ms. Edgewater, and Tara, even the boys who had left him to die in the blackness of the alleyway. All of them. His grandmother, his parents, Anna, whose love he had never forgotten. And the new friend who shared his father's first name, but who preferred to be known as Gravity. He was at one with all of them. Cirrus Jacobs would travel to the other side of the doorway with all of their essences embedded within his heart and mind.

Nimbus tried to scream, but Cirrus's will held him back. He remembered a time when he had been laying in bed watching TV when he noticed some rather peculiar movements on the floor beneath the window. When his eyes focused on the cause of the movement, he found it to be the most enormous spider he had ever seen. It had somehow grown unnoticed by the laws of nature and thus escaped the directives that governed normalcy within the animal kingdom. Cirrus felt no fear at the beginning, because he had never before been afraid of spiders or insects. Cirrus had trapped the spider's body inside a transparent drinking glass, and held it up to the table. Its disproportionate body made his muscles tremble with uncertainty. Its hairy fangs were, by normal insect standards, gargantuan in perspective. Cirrus was sure that it, too, must have somehow escaped from the darkened pathways of another dimension; perhaps he had followed Cirrus out when he narrowly escaped the mist.

As he held the spider's imprisoned body into the light, it made no movement. Perhaps it was trying to convince him that maybe he had perished from the lack of oxygen. Cirrus was certain that it would be able to survive in the glass for weeks, but its stillness was so utterly convincing.

When after an hour of apparent lifelessness had passed, Jacobs tapped at the glass with his fingers. As if a bolt of electricity possessed it, the spider's gangly legs sprung to life, and it ran in circles around the perimeter of its prison cell. The movement inside of the glass looked like a hurricane of brown and blackness. The spider ran for several minutes, until Cirrus outwitted him into a trip down the toilet. Even after he saw the last of its legs disappear down the drain, Cirrus's fear remained at full attention. Just in case the spider crawled its way out during the middle of the night.

Nimbus behaved this way now. Cirrus's spine shivered as he felt him trying to break free. Like the spider, Nimbus, too, ran in circles around his cell. He had grown teeth and they shattered in his mouth as he tried to use them to chew through the cold steel bars of his confinement. Cirrus's mind throbbed in physical pain as Nimbus bore his weight against the sides of his mind. Cirrus Jacobs stood upon his perch, head back, and arms extended to his sides like Jesus Christ himself.

Below him was a two-hundred-foot drop into darkness. At the center of this uncertainty was the doorway. It was time for all of his secrets to be revealed, a time to come to grips with his reality. It was for both the benefit of those that would find him, as well as his own.

The walls of his world were rapidly falling to the ground and they could no longer sustain any more darkness. Let the light flood the universe and cast the shadows into hiding forever, let them wash down the drain. What really was Paradoxum?

It was a place where existence had no physical sense, where time remained unmeasured. Paradoxum lived within the deepest recesses of the mind, where one went to hope. To travel there was effortless. It was the place you went to dream, to desire, to process logic, and to reason. It was a matter of closing the eyes and allowing for the natural drift. This mystic place could be encountered during deep sleep when rapid eye movement occurred, or in moments when emotion reigned supreme over intellect. It was the place two people visited together when they were locked in each other's embrace. A place that became visible at moments when intense heat was generated between two bodies that breathed in complete unison, becoming one.

It was the place that Cirrus Jacobs's had created inside his mind because he could no longer handle living here, in your world. There was only one way to reach this place, through the most inevitable of all places: death. He had known it then as he had always known it. Since Cirrus had sat alone on the floor of his apartment where his walk had begun. He did not want to think about it at the time, but it was inescapable now. He had decided to walk to try and find some goodness to live for. Perhaps his destiny was to be found in his desperation.

By what means and at what time and location Cirrus Jacobs would leave had been unknown to him. Although he had felt a sense of insanity throughout, it was a means of hiding away what he knew was the foreseeable. He had felt an impulse to end his life early, to his surprise, in the alleyway when the truck would have torn his body in two. It was Nimbus who pushed him out of the way.

The fear of facing death was not an easy thing for the mind to grasp, and Cirrus had began talking to himself internally to help him cope. Nimbus was his conscience, and he had always known how it was going to end. It seemed he had always been living within reality and fooled himself into believing there was an escape.

Throughout his life, Cirrus had been hanging on a rope with his bloodied hands. Every day, the fibers withered away even further, until that moment, when there was but a single strand holding him in this world of yours. In a moment, the last fiber would snap, and he would wave goodbye to all of the darkness that had shrouded him for so long. He had wanted to stay. Jacobs tried so desperately to see some goodness, to see some purity. His arguments with Nimbus had revolved around this sole topic. He had been living an existence of fear, and the day he realized that he would have to accept a life without love, was the day he had decided to commit this terrible act. But he was not afraid.

He would face this moment as he had been forced to face everything else in his life, with strength. The kind of fearlessness that no man had witnessed before. What was there to be so afraid of? What was death, really, but a return to birth? The world turned before his entrance, as it would continue to turn after his departure. Cirrus's memories of prebirth were nonexistent. There was no pain or sorrow to feel; there was nothing. And so shall it would be after death; it had to be. It was but a mere cycle. There was nothing to hang onto before birth and that's what would be difficult when he died. It would be unbearable to take that pain with him. But he was certain that those things did not thrive in Paradoxum. It was a place of beauty; the kind of splendor he had witnessed as a child. Through the doorway below, he would return to that innocence.

Nimbus had warned him earlier about the consequences of his decision. He had warned of what lay beyond the borders of afterlife; he had understood it was discussed for centuries. It was said that if one should choose to take his own life, he would be subjected to eternal damnation. To live an eternity of suffering for punishment for what he had done. Cirrus didn't believe any of that; never had. Even if there was only a slight chance of crossing over into the world of purity that he knew resided in Paradoxum, he was willing to take that chance.

What was death, but a transference of energy from one earthly shell to another? The soul lived forever, and only changed from one identity and time to another. Where could it go? At the moment of his death, he would awaken somewhere else, oblivious to what had unfolded before the present time. He could no longer live with the constant ache in his heart.

Every human being went through ebbs and flows of loss and depression, he knew this. He had approached every angle with logic, but could not recall a time when there was an absence of the uncertainty. The fear and the sadness. The insight came not from Nimbus, but from himself. Through his voice Cirrus knew; he had tried to reason himself out of taking a step he could never cross back over, but he had finalized his decision long ago.

"Do not do this," Nimbus's voice hissed, choking his words through the blood and broken teeth in his mouth.

"You have made your way free, I see."

"I have given you every reason to stay. Now you must think rationally. You are needed here; there is a duty which goes unfulfilled."

"How did you break free of your cell?" Cirrus asked calmly, looking toward the doorway below. He gritted his teeth and pushed Nimbus further below.

Still, his voice came through the void of Cirrus's single broken tooth. "There is no prison you can create that can keep me hidden. I do not sleep. There is no return. That place below contains only darkness. There is no light to be found down there, Cirrus, not if you willingly walk into its grip. It will take you when it is your time and there will be light, I assure you of this. But not today, my dear boy. Today it is not meant for you."

Cirrus opened his eyes. "Today, my friend, you are free. Go, and let me fall in peace."

"Today is not meant for you!" Nimbus screamed.

The sounds came rushing out of his head and into the nature that surrounded him. Unexplainably, it echoed between the mountainous landscape. The realization came quickly. It was the sound of his own voice, and not that of Nimbus. It seemed Cirrus Jacobs had finally broken, like his shoes. Cirrus had begun doing what he had never wanted to hear himself doing, uttering phrases into the wind where there were only phantoms to listen. The echo circled around for another pass, scaring birds out of their nests and into flight. *"Today is not meant for you!"* The snow began to fall in flurries from the clouds.

"Goodbye, my friend," Cirrus said to his only companion.

Nimbus responded furiously through Cirrus's own mouth. "Paradoxum is not yours to claim!"

Nimbus screamed like a wolf inside Jacobs's mind, but he cast the voice aside. He did not stop. Cirrus only repeated himself and realized with deep sadness it would be the last words he would speak. "Goodbye, my friend."

Arms still outstretched, he turned to look below. The light had filled the canyon and he could now see his final destination. No one would find him there. Perhaps when the snow had melted, they would find his belongings. Inside his backpack, they would find what was left of his earthly existence. A roll of photographic memories from his final days, and his identification, which bore his image as he had looked before he had been clutched into the icy grip of darkness.

Tears rolled along his cheeks, and he was unable to make them stop. He felt so utterly alone. There was only silence around him, and even the birds had stopped their cries of warning. Below, there were only three colors he could see. The reddish-grey of rocks, green from the flora that flourished below, and the white of snow. His eyes would be filled with this simplicity when he burned his final image. As the snow covered his body, the cold attempted to weaken him even further. Steam rose from his skin into the frigid oxygen, and he could taste its sweetness. The air smelled clean and pure, the kind of purity he had so longed for in Paradoxum, and one that he found now only when he was leaving. The clean snow melted into his mouth and as Cirrus looked through his blurred tears, his eyes were filled with images of the pure white clouds in the horizon.

One of them was strangely out of place on that lonely winter morning. It was out of season, the kind that only showed itself in the strawberry sunsets of late summer when the air was warm with sunlight. A cirrus cloud, like the kind a man might see when he was resting on his front porch, drinking an ice-cold beer and listening lovingly to his wife as she spoke about her day.

Cirrus leaned forward and let the weight of his body shift forward. The balls of his heels slowly began to disconnect from the concrete median he stood on. As the gap between the concrete and his bare feet widened, Cirrus Jacobs closed his eyes and let himself be swallowed by the silence. His lungs inhaled a deep breath of air and trapped it there, desperate to hold on to one last breath. There was only the sound of his beating heart as gravity began to pull him home. Cirrus forced his lungs to exhale the last breath and he closed his eyes.

The warriors of Darkness and Light began their battle.

*   *   *

Emily Porter entered with the slam of her car door. Raymond spoke to her over his shoulder as he played with the baby. "All done, babe?"

"All done," she said, strapping on her seatbelt. "I put two creams and two sweeteners in it. They were all out of sugar."

"Were the people strange in there?" he asked.

"What do you mean by that?"

"I mean these small-town folk are weird sometimes. Did you see that guy on the way up here? He looked like a madman wandering the streets."

"Just because he looked a little shaggy and was walking by himself, doesn't mean that there's something wrong with him."

Ray thought about this for a moment and then responded. "I guess, Em, but something was not right about him. I think he was arguing with himself. I saw his lips moving."

"We're only about two hours away from the city, right?" she said. "I think that the closer we get, the more normal people become."

Raymond began to back the car out of the last service station they would hit before he surprised his wife with their apartment. When he depressed the brake lever, the car slid slightly in the snow. "Whoa, babe, be careful," said Emily. She unfolded the paperback novel to the last page she had left it on. "It's slippery."

"I know, these are good tires, though," Raymond said while he turned the wheel sharply to the right. He merged back onto the main road. He wouldn't have pulled into yet another small town if Emily hadn't had to use the washroom, although the town they had stopped in wasn't that small to begin with. That particular town had many more people occupying its streets than any of the ones they had stopped in previously. Raymond was glad, as a matter of fact, to reunite with civilization again. The only down side was they had to travel twenty minutes on a side road up the mountainside to get there.

From the back road to the heart of the town, there was nothing but rock and forest. That was where Raymond had seen the lone traveler walking up the slope. *Poor guy*, Raymond had thought. *Probably worked his hands to the bone and couldn't even afford a decent car to go home with.*

He had tried to create a background story for the man, one that he might be able to recreate in his novel, but the stranger kept his head low and didn't provide many details with which Raymond could work. In fact, Raymond had only noticed three things: a dirty yellow raincoat with a hood that covered most of the man's face; worn black shoes that seemed to be in such an advanced state of wear, that they looked to be falling off his feet; and the last thing he noticed was the man's lips moving to himself. He had only been joking with Emily, because even he had caught himself talking to no one in particular every now and again.

The Porter family car rolled effortlessly down the mountainside, back toward the highway. As Raymond had predicted, the snow tires gripped the road with perfect authority. They kicked up snow in their wake, but as a precaution, Raymond slowed his speed.

The radio had sung its final song for the day. Basking in the silence, Julia napped in the safety of her car seat while Emily's pupils dilated with every sentence of anticipation she read in her book. Raymond concentrated on the road, anxious to reach their destination. He turned to speak to his wife. "I ever mention how much I love you?"

With surprise, Emily looked over and answered. "All the time."

"Good," he said. "Just thought I'd let you know. Maybe I don't say it enough, but I think about it every second. It's important that you know that. That's the truth."

Her last sentence hung in midair. "I know you do, Ray, I ..."

The car had gained an equal distance between the mountain road and the town behind them when suddenly Raymond inadvertently drove over a large rock protruding from the road. Had he passed this rock less than fifteen minutes ago, he would have seen it lying in wait for the events that were to follow.

As the snow fell like a blanket from the clouds, the rock's bright red face had been covered by a sheet of whiteness that Raymond would have found an impossibility to avoid. When the rock struck the tire with its strong foothold embedded into the bedrock below, it loosened a shard of amber glass that had somehow lodged itself into the black rubber tread of Raymond's Volkswagen tire.

As the glass was expelled into the snow behind, the hole that it left spread open like a suddenly opened fist. It exploded with the force of dynamite. Thick chunks of black rubber spewed onto the perfection of the white snow. Raymond locked his arms into position around the wheel as Emily turned to hold the car seat steady with her arm. Miraculously, in the midst of all that was unfolding, Julia remained asleep. The red crayon was clenched tightly in her hand.

No one in the car made a sound. It was an eerie tranquility that could perhaps only be found within the nothingness of outer space.

A silence so profound, that one might have deduced that all of the activity in the world had momentarily come to an abrupt halt.

Although Raymond forced the wheel to comply within his grasp, the car's remaining systems jammed under his control. As the brakes locked, the car turned sharply to the right and pushed its heavy metal body down the slope like an out of control bobsledder. Emily was gritting her teeth, holding on to the baby's seat with one hand, and Raymond's neck with her other. He felt her support pass through his skin, and fought harder than ever to regain control.

Like a freight train, the car slid completely sideways, closer toward the curve at the bottom of the road. Raymond looked through the driver's side window and saw their path in direct trajectory to the cliff's edge. His mind calculated faster than it had ever worked before. The only way to stop the car from going over the edge was to somehow slide its back end in a complete 360-degree circle until they slammed into the side of the rock face, where the road curved around.

His voice shook with the rumble from the road. "Emily!" he screamed. "Hang on! Hold Julia!"

Emily Porter reacted even quicker than her husband made his calculations and tensed her body for the impact. At that moment, the mathematical laws of time and space rippled and slowed to a sloth's pace. The animals, which had hidden within their carefully protected homes, scurried out to witness what made the great noise.

Raymond thumped on the brake as hard as he could when the car reached precisely the right place, and jerked the wheel to the right to force its collision with the rocks. His logic being that a slam into the wall and a *chance* at survival would be better than certain death over the cliff. He bit on his lip so hard that blood came oozing out of the freshly cut flesh. He tasted it as it washed over his tongue. The fingernails on his hands dug deeply into the soft plastic meat that made up the steering wheel. As Raymond's knee bobbed up and down on the brake, the sounds of the interaction filled the car's interior. The silence, which had previously occupied this space, was forced out by the rumbling of the entire car. It danced on its shocks as it glided down the hill at the mercy of whatever forces had decided to step in.

Emily closed her eyes and prayed. In an instant, she begged angrily for her little girl to be spared. Raymond heard her when she asked out loud, and he, too, begged for their lives. The car became covered in snow as it fell, catching the tops of unstable treetops as it passed. Branches and twigs snapped loudly as it descended, crushing everything in its path.

Like a snowplow Raymond's side of the car threw massive blankets of white over its roof, where it landed on Emily's side and rested gently onto the road. Through the view from his window, only whiteness. Through hers, the remains of their path, like Raymond's faded memories. A branch of shrubbery washed against Raymond's window.

He was now braced with his wife nestled in his chest, both of them stretching their seatbelts to maximum capacity in the center. Each of them held a section of their daughter's seat, and still, she slept like a lake on a warm summer morning. Their muscles tensed in unison because the snow blocked their view. In those few seconds, it had occurred to Raymond that they might have already plummeted over the edge. There was no way to tell.

When the shrub brushed against the window, it cleared a fist-sized field of vision into the world outside. What Raymond Porter saw was a scene, even in the middle of this madness, that made his heart sink.

A man stood alone at the threshold between land and air, arms outstretched. It was the same man he had seen earlier, when they had driven past. He had stripped himself of his clothes from the waist up, and was now leaning forward into the falling snow. It seemed the world had slowed its pace even outside of the car. Raymond could see the space created between the concrete and his bare feet, and the man's body beginning to glide into the air he was falling into.

He held his wife's head in his chest and witnessed the edge getting closer and closer. Raymond Porter's hand found Julia's inside of the chaos, and he held her tiny fingers gently in his. Sadness filled him and for the first time in an eternity, his wife saw tears roll down his face. Even when Julia was born, he had hid them from her. Now they rained down hurriedly, landing droplets onto his wife's hand.

At this, she looked inside his deep, brown eyes and kissed them from her skin, whispering words into his ear and finishing her last sentence, a sentence that had been suddenly interrupted. "I love you, too."

Raymond's eyes filled with grey. The last thing he saw before the car was slammed into the median was the shade of concrete pressing into the car. It encompassed his entire world and washed over him like a sigh. Then there was nothing.

A moment prior, a single thought had occupied his mind: that he had seen that color before. Where, he could not recall; only that he was sure he had seen it before. Perhaps in a long forgotten dream. It was as if his insight into the universe were covered in paint, like a child's hand had brushed a stroke of watercolor across his eyes.

And in his heart, he longed for the bright yellow of sunshine.

*   *   *

Cirrus did not hear anything at first, not until he opened his eyes. From behind, the sound barrier was broken. Something caused a rumble deep in the earth and it found him, there at the edge. If one were to assume the cause of the trembling, one might have assumed a thousand bears were running down the mountainside in perfect synchronicity. Something with such force, it had pushed heavy air alongside the left side of his face, causing the wet skin to drop a few degrees.

Palms open and arms outstretched, like a bird he stood. Cirrus leaned forward, let destiny take its course. The darkened nature of his own humanity pulled him closer to the doorway, inch by inch. The wind on his face broke his concentration and Cirrus had been forced to open his eyes and see the horror which lay before him.

A car, or what used to be a car, teetered over the edge of the cliff. Somehow, as if he had cheated the laws of gravity, his body hung in limbo somewhere between ground and air. Cirrus Jacobs did not feel the impact of what had landed beside him, and surely under normal circumstances, it would have sent him tumbling forward down into the black chasm. But today was no ordinary day. Here and now was no ordinary place. That day, the boundaries between dimensions had opened and natural laws were certainly not applicable there.

The mass of twisted metal tipped dangerously forward, its front end mashed beyond recognition. It faced down over the edge of the cliff in an almost ninety-degree angle. As he turned his head, Cirrus's inner mind whispered to the only one who would listen.

"Nimbus, help me ..."

There was no response. The car leaned in an angle matched exactly by his own body and at any moment, either one of them could go over the edge by the push of a hair. Only an instant had passed since the collision had occurred. Cirrus's energy was drawn by his mind; the whirlwind was stronger than it had ever been, and suddenly, his body was pushed backward.

It felt as if someone had clenched his claws around his waist and pulled him back. He landed with a vicious *THUD!* in the ever-deepening snow. Cirrus's skin began to melt it on contact. He was momentarily dumbfounded at having cheated the natural laws that governed the universe. How was one to accept such a thing? That somehow he had fallen backward instead of forward when the impact happened. Somehow his balance reacted in an opposite reaction.

Had a magnet pulled him back? Jacobs's frail bones trembled at the sight in front of him. Silence enveloped the air. He watched helplessly as the car tipped forward even further. Nimbus's voice suddenly echoed through the walls of the strange world in which they stood. Only two words, over and over.

"Get up! Get up! Get up!"

Confusion blindsided his senses and he glanced around through blurry vision, mouth open wide in awe. Cirrus's muscles froze because he didn't know what to do. From the car, there was a sound. Crying.

Like a sweet song, her voice traveled through the air and danced into his ear. The sounds miraculously fed him energy and began to clear the clouds that saturated his mind. In one single moment his legs rose from the whiteness of the snow, as if her voice was giving him encoded instructions.

Abruptly, the car became engulfed in flames. Black smoke poured from its underside in thick billows as its weight shifted evermore toward the emptiness below. Clarity and strength filled Cirrus Jacobs's being. Control possessed his legs and he ran toward the wreck, oblivious to the heat and smoke. Through gritted teeth, he breathed the blackness and forced it to fill him with more strength. The heat, which singed the trees and turned the snow into flowing water, gave his muscles hope. Finally, after what seemed like days, he reached the car.

Inside the backseat was a baby, whose cries had penetrated through the steel and smoke. Hands shaking, Cirrus opened the back door.

Grey and black smoke leached out like escapees from a prison riot. It burned his eyes, but somehow his vision remained crystal clear.

She sat in a car seat, strapped safely within webs of seatbelts. In her hand, she held a red crayon. The sight filled Cirrus with both joy and sadness at once. As he looked to the front of the car from the inside, he could only see crumpled metal. From the length of the tip of the hood, to the back seat. This space had been reduced down to two feet of mangled and blackened metal, burning with every second that passed. His nose filled with the smell of melting plastic and burning gasoline.

Absolute sadness filled him as he looked to the baby, who had stopped crying. She looked at the sight of a man hanging halfway in the car, and staring blankly at what used to be the front seat of a car. He felt a profound emptiness fill his chest, and one that he could not explain. A concrete lump formed in his throat.

At that moment, he was revisiting his own demons. Looking at his own childhood, at his own parents who had perished in a car wreck. Looking back through Paradoxum. But he was not.

The smells that had risen into his brain told him immediately how real it actually was, the clearly identifiable smell of burning flesh. The lump in his throat blocked his airway and loosened itself into his eyes where tears broke free of their ducts. He wept loudly and uncontrollably at what he knew, but could not accept, had happened. Cirrus's fingers worked independently of his brain and his heart, and unlocked the belts which harnessed her little body.

He picked her body up gently in his arms and pushed back against the car. The smoke in the front seat belched, and for a split second, cleared enough to cast one last image into his vision. He saw two hands, interlocking fingers, and a glowing wedding ring on each. Then the smoke swallowed the remainder of the car.

Cirrus Jacobs ran with the baby in his arms and was forced to turn as the ground beneath his feet began to tremble. The car began its final salute and tipped forward with the weight of the flames. It was as if the baby's tiny body had provided just enough counter-balance to keep the car from falling. Once he had removed her, he had forever shifted consequence. The black mass rose into the air and stood for a moment, completely vertical. Like a person performing a swan dive, the car hurdled itself down the mountainside and into the blackness. Into Paradoxum.

Cirrus Jacobs lay his back against the rock face with the baby's warm body against his. The snow around him had turned to black. From the chasm below, a monstrosity of smoke billowed into the clouds. So far down that he didn't even hear a crash. Perhaps a doorway had swallowed the sound. He looked at the baby, who lay calmly in his arms. Her wide eyes glowed with curiosity and she shook her arms at him, still clutching the crayon in her tiny fingers. Cirrus tried to control his tears because he knew she was trying to say thanks.

Sirens cut through the air. He waited for their arrival with his eyes closed, as the snow fell gently from the clouds. The baby, too, closed her eyes.

They waited as the earth began to revolve at its normal pace and the natural laws that governed the universe took their place. All was returned back to reality.

Chapter Thirteen

The girl who sat silently next to the window was a part of who Cirrus was, and who he would become. She was the light that he had always been searching for. Her name was Julia, and she was the daughter of Raymond and Emily Porter. They met through the strangest of circumstances, a situation that was so perfectly timed that one would not believe the story if one were not to believe in fate.

Cirrus Jacobs sat on the front stoop of his apartment building, sipping hot coffee. The liquid poured through the empty space in his mouth, a place where a tooth had once occupied. It stood as a reminder of where he had just escaped.

Children played in the distance, laughing and hollering their way to school. And you know what? It brought a smile to his face. A face that hadn't smiled in decades, it seemed. His friend John Everett sat quietly beside him, and they enjoyed the scene together. Cars drove slowly down the street and honked their horns at neighbors, waving greetings to each other with grins.

When he had returned back to his beloved city, Cirrus visited the only place he knew and the only one he knew, John Everett. When John arrived at the door, he didn't seem surprised at Cirrus's appearance; he merely opened the door and let him in. Without a word John handed him a towel, a razor, and some clothes. Cirrus walked into the bathroom and began cleaning himself of the filth that had penetrated into his skin over the course of his life. When he emerged from the clean steam of the washroom, John asked him only one question. If he had learned to breathe. Cirrus told him that yes, indeed he had.

It was funny how a life could come full circle, where a journey would end in the same place it had begun. But what could be learned during the process was what was important. Cirrus began walking to search for the light. He had learned that light came not in the form of a flood one day, but gathered itself over time.

*   *   *

Cirrus had been home for three weeks. John had been kind enough to let Cirrus stay with him for a few days, and then announced that he had spoken to the manager and secured his old apartment for him. Jacobs felt like he'd been gone for years, but in reality, it had been six days. John handed him the key and sent him across the hall with an envelope of cash and a box. Inside the box there were various items; the most important: a gold watch.

Cirrus stepped into the room and inhaled the familiar air. The blinds were closed and the walls had been freshly painted. No more ghosts clinging to the walls. He walked over to the window and opened the blinds, where for the first time in months sunlight poured through. The light brightened the entire room, and he opened the window to feel its warmth against his skin. It was indescribable.

Cirrus took a walk every day, by the same rhythmic pattern as when he searched for his dream world. The difference being, he always returned home. As he walked, he breathed, gathering up bits of light that he came across. Cirrus stored them in his mind, next to the darkness. He had learned that both elements were crucial for survival. There was a frail balance between the two, and one could not survive without the other. They did not battle, but coexisted. He'd have his bad days, but not like before. When he breathed the air, he basked in its taste. When colors penetrated his iris, he remembered their every hue.

A man must be stripped of everything before he can realize what he is in actual possession of. He had to remind himself to remember those things every day, and if he should forget, the pictures he had fastened to the wall would be a constant reminder.

Opposite from the window where the sun painted the walls every day, was a photographic image of Jake the dog resting beneath a tree. There was the spirit of Charlie's empty chair and the mesmerizing architecture of the church. Cirrus's struggle at the base of the *Realization*

Tree, and of course Tara, Ms. Edgewater, and Gravity, even Julia. Many pictures now hung on the wall, the last of which was a man whom he barely recognized anymore. The man's skin was as thin as a ghoul, face unshaven, and one tooth missing. So much could be said about a portrait taken in black-and-white, but this time, the eyes told a story that was far too painful to recall.

The innocence of Cirrus's childhood had been returned and Julia had shown him where he belonged in the world. Through the strange imbalance of destiny, he found his place. Cirrus Jacobs now knew how fragile a single breath could be, and those ghosts who haunted his mind had been returned to their place, along with his friend Nimbus.

Cirrus felt his presence with him always, but Nimbus's words had been silenced. Instead, it was the sound of his own voice, the sound of his own direction. On one horribly fateful day, a day when the world seemed to stop, two beautiful souls were taken away. They left behind all of their hopes, ambitions, and love in the form of their daughter Julia. She had been returned to her home as well, returned with love into the arms of her uncle Barry and the rest of her family. Raymond and Emily's spirit lived within Julia, as Cirrus's own family history lived within him. All was not lost. With their tragic death, came the rebirth of another.

Cirrus sat in the warm, still morning, soaking in the sun that had been absent for so long. Its rays were blinding and he smiled as he looked to the sky. High above there was only blue, save for one small blur of white. A lazy cloud stretched its body across the sky, flowing with the wind. In its wisps, freedom was personified. Like a dream, this cirrus cloud floated, smiling down to him. It passed in front of the sun and let free a beam that caught a sparkle of light from an object below. The light danced irregular shapes on the brick face of the buildings across the street.

What shone along the walls of the building was the rebirth of Cirrus Jacobs. It was the shimmering of his father's gold watch that rested proudly upon his wrist.

Epilogue

A man named Rodney sat cross-legged on an upturned milk crate, smoking a cigarette. He looked to the scene in front of him with lazy, dreamy eyes. The smoke from the cigarette in his hand swirled around his neck. He wore a white apron and a dishwasher's uniform, a pair of orange rubber gloves tucked within the strings of his apron. He thought about many things. He thought of how he hadn't seen an old acquaintance of his in some time. A man named Gravity, who usually came around to say hello from time to time, had not been seen in several days.

The dishwasher hoped he was all right. He hoped for many things, as he always had. Rodney sat not at the back loading dock of a hotel, but somewhere within the confines of his mind. He looked straight ahead, where there was an alleyway filled with the backsides of buildings and garbage bins.

The young man did not see the filth of the street in his mind's eye, but instead a beautiful tropical landscape. Rodney's vivid imagination had transported him out of the routine world that he had grown accustomed to, and dropped him on a warm beach facing the magnificent blue waters of the Pacific Ocean. A hidden smile hid beneath his expression as he enjoyed the view. Suddenly, the back door of the employee's entrance opened and a man in a tall chef's hat stepped out.

"Hey, Rod, you almost done with your break?" he said.

The chef spoke again as the dishwasher provided no response. "The banquet will be over in five minutes, so we'll need you upstairs."

Taking a drag of his cigarette and closing off the portal to his tropical realm, Rodney replied, "I'll be right up."

The chef disappeared behind the doors again and Rodney stood, curls of smoke blowing from his nostrils. He turned to take one last look at the scene before it was magically shaken back into a grungy and stinky alleyway. He slid the orange gloves over his hands and reached for the doorknob, when there was a voice. It came from behind the bins, down both sides of the street, from under the milk crate on which he sat. He turned to find its owner, searching with his eyes from side to side.

The voice slithered from the street. "Afraid of what lies before you? Rather see something else, my boy? I can help you."

The muscles between the dishwasher's eyes tensed as he lowered his head and looked for the source of the snaky voice. Rodney shouted into the alleyway. "Who's there?"

A voice responded immediately, as if it had been waiting for the question. Its every word slithered over the dishwasher's skin. "Look to the ground, to your shadow … that is where I dwell."

Confused, Rodney asked again, "Who are you?"

The response came quickly, like it had been trapped inside his mind. The voice came through the walls and made the hair on his arms stand beneath the rubber gloves. A rake passed over his spine in a shiver when the answer was given.

"I am you, of course."

Confusion filled the dishwasher's head like tear gas and he closed his eyes. He tried to send himself back to the warmth of the tropical landscape that dwelled in his mind, trying to silence the voice, but he could not focus.

"I am you," the voice calmly repeated. "I am you."

THE END

A Note from the Author

The term *coincidence* must be explored here to some extent in determining how this concept was used in defining some of the circumstances found "coincidentally" in *Paradox and Rebirth*.

There are conditions in life that can act as catalysts in directing one's own personal journey through certain points of existence. Situations that could be classified as miraculous could go overlooked. In contrast, events that seem mundane to some could have profound effects on others. How one perceives the events at hand determines how one might react to them. It is how these situations are viewed, and through how many different sets of eyes are projected upon the events. What types of backgrounds and insights do each of us bring to the table?

There are countless instances of coincidence floating around us, and only until they are discussed and investigated, do we pluck their secrets out of thin air. Many of us behave in similar ways and react in similar forms. We do many of the same types of things that we may consider to be private. Thoughts that roll around in our heads about who we are and what types of things stand to be discovered in our futures are indeed shared by many.

There are many coincidences contained within the pages of this story that need to be further scrutinized to provide a better sense of understanding for the reader. What those coincidences are, I will let you discover. The occurrences and similarities between Cirrus Jacobs and Raymond Porter were incorporated into the story to illustrate only one point: that there is a connection these two men shared on some kind of strange cosmic level. Both men long for the same things in life. One attains these things, and the other is tortured without them. It is my attempt to explore the lives of two men who are cut from the same cloth, but lead very different lives as a result.

Lastly, I wanted to provide some notes on what defines *hope* and the role it plays on the life of Cirrus Jacobs. Here is a man who looks for hope his entire life and finds it only when he has finally conceded and given up looking for it. How many of us haven't laid sleepless at one time or another, arguing with our own inner voices? Which one of us can say we haven't spent some time in our own personal versions of *Paradoxum,* imagining better things?

If for no other reason, hope itself can provide the only motivation to take another step forward. It would be wise to give it that consideration just for curiosity's sake. How else are we to know what forces cast light just beyond the corner? Is it salvation, or could it just be Nimbus returning for another conversation?

If that step is not taken, how will we ever know?